Warm, male and vibrantly alive

She was conscious only of the sweetness of his mouth, the feel of him. But then, even as her knees began to buckle, the anger reasserted itself. The world was filled with her own ragged, indrawn breath.

"How dare you."

"Very easily."

He seemed perfectly unruffled, which inflamed her anger further. And yet—was he? There was a dusky flush along his hard-edged cheekbones, a tautness around his mouth, that suggested— Carly closed her mind to what it suggested and, summoning all her depleted resources, thrust her chin proudly in the air.

"I think you'd better go, don't you?" She used the special voice that she kept in the freezer compartment of her fridge, specifically for dealing with men like this, and he responded instantly.

RACHEL FORD was born in Coventry, descended from a long line of Warwickshire farmers. She met her husband at Birmingham University, and he is now a principal lecturer in a polytechnic school. Rachel and her husband both taught school in the West Indies for several years after their marriage, and have had fabulous holidays in Mexico, as well as unusual experiences in Venezuela and Ecuador during revolutions and coups! Their two daughters were born in England. After stints as a teacher and information guide, Rachel took up writing, which she really enjoys doing the most—first children's and girls' stories, and finally, romance novels.

Books by Rachel Ford

HARLEQUIN PRESENTS
1160—A SHADOWED LOVE
1304—LOVE'S FUGITIVE
1337—WEB OF DESIRE
1368—LORD OF THE FOREST
1402—AFFAIR IN BIARRITZ
1424—RHAPSODY OF LOVE
1479—MAN OF ROCK

HARLEQUIN ROMANCE
2913—CLOUDED PARADISE
3116—LOVE'S AWAKENING

RACHEL FORD

The Iron Master

Harlequin Books

TORONTO • NEW YORK • LONDON
AMSTERDAM • PARIS • SYDNEY • HAMBURG
STOCKHOLM • ATHENS • TOKYO • MILAN
MADRID • WARSAW • BUDAPEST • AUCKLAND

With thanks to the management of the
Boro Foundry Ltd, Lye, West Midlands,
for their help in the preparation
of this book

ISBN 0-373-11654-3

THE IRON MASTER

Printed in U.S.A.

CHAPTER ONE

CARLY half got to her feet as the door beside her burst open. The new arrival, a man—a large man, she amended—was loaded down with files and a huge brown cardboard box, on which was perched a bulging briefcase. As he went to close the door with his elbow, the case slid from its precarious perch and went crashing to the floor.

'Oh, let me help.'

Jumping up instinctively to retrieve it, she cannoned violently into its owner as he swung round and sent the stack of files flying.

'For crying out loud!'

A scowl came from beneath the shock of unruly black curls, then as, crimson-faced, she mumbled an apology and began scrabbling the files together, he brusquely pushed her aside with a, 'Leave it to me. I don't want the entire place wrecked.'

As she backed away, he gathered up his possessions into a neat balancing act and, leaving Carly no more than an aggrieved spectator, was heading on towards the office door when it opened. The pretty young woman, heavily pregnant, whom Carly had seen when she first arrived, over an hour earlier, put her head round it.

'Ah, good, you're here.'

'Yes, I am—at last.' Another black scowl. 'Can I help it if the whole bloody air traffic system between Sydney and Heathrow went into instant rigor mortis the moment I set foot on the plane? Anyway, now I'm here I've got——'

7

'Nick, this is——'

'——these figures I want you to type up straight away——'

'But, Nick——'

'——and can you tell Giles and Ray that I want to see them here at ten-thirty.' And he was gone, without even a halfway backward glance in her direction.

Well, of all the uncouth, overbearing swine! Carly, expelling a long, angry breath, gave the wooden panels a baleful glare. Men. They were all alike. This—*tornado* who'd just swept through had the same look about him as her new boss, and she'd spent the weekend smarting from the painful session she'd had with him the previous Friday.

'Now, Miss Sheppard, perhaps you'd be good enough to clarify this for me.'

Dr Jutson tossed the letter across the desk at her. Carly unfolded it, saw the embossed heading 'Milton Education Authority', then, with a steadily sinking heart, skipped through it, her eye picking out the incriminating phrases: '...remind you that the first interim report is now due...member of your staff, Miss Caroline Sheppard...secondment for temporary part-time industrial experience...'

'Well?' The rimless glasses were regarding her expressionlessly.

'Er——' She floundered to a halt under the silent inquisition.

'It appears from this letter that since September you have been seconded for two days a week to Bradley and Son, Ironfounders. Correct me, of course, if I'm wrong——' you know you aren't, damn you, Carly thought '——but this term you do not appear to have been absent from Milton Community College for two hours, much less two days per week.'

'That's right,' she agreed reluctantly.

'I know nothing of this arrangement, you understand. Perhaps you can enlighten me.'

'Well,' she said slowly, 'it was fixed up at the end of last term, just before Miss Davis retired. The chairman of the education committee got this bee in his bonnet— I mean,' she corrected herself hastily, 'he had this idea about teachers spending six months part-time in the local factories and so on, where their pupils would end up. And Miss Davis volunteered me to go to Bradley's, to shadow one of the members of staff there.'

No need to add that last July she'd wriggled and squirmed desperately to get out of it. Having spent the whole year building up a really good, close relationship with her remedial class of fifteen-year-olds, she had been frantic not to hand them over to another teacher for nearly half the week. 'Carly's Thugs' was how the rest of the staff derisively referred to 5S and, heaven knew it had taken long enough to get some of them out of their shells and responding to her blend of kindness and firmness, so that she didn't want to risk all that work being destroyed.

She'd hoped that, with the change of principal, the scheme would slip through the bureaucratic net and be forgotten. Even so, the first week of term she'd tensed every time anyone knocked on her classroom door, but when the summons hadn't come it had gradually faded from her mind. Now it had blown up in her face.

'So, why have you not been?'

'I—I thought I was more useful here.' She hated the placatory tone in her voice. For two pins, she'd get up now, tell this—this desiccated dictator, who was rapidly turning the happy atmosphere of Milton Community

College into one of tense joylessness, what she thought of him, and slam in her notice to take effect from Christmas. But that would mean leaving her class, and she couldn't—wouldn't do that, not for any head in the whole of Yorkshire.

'Oh, we're none of us indispensable, Miss Sheppard.' The heavy irony set her teeth on edge. 'You're still very young, of course. What is it—twenty-four? You have yet to learn that the world will roll onwards without us—and the fifth-year remedial class of this college will still turn on its axis if you're absent for two days a week.'

'Yes, I understand that, Dr Jutson. But——'

'May I remind you——' for the first time, Carly registered the spots of mottled, angry colour on his cheekbones '—that, under the terms of your contract, you are expected to fulfil all reasonable duties that the principal might require of you.'

Carly's lips tightened as she met the cold gaze from behind the lenses. All reasonable duties... Very soon after his arrival, the principal had made it clear, in the subtlest of ways, of course, that he would be more than interested in any little extra-mural activities she might care to join him in, but she had made it equally clear that she did not return that interest—not with him, or any other man, for that matter. Since then, he'd retaliated with a continual campaign of petty sniping—so this débâcle would be manna from heaven, as far as he was concerned.

'If you'll kindly wait outside, I'll ring Bradley's, apologise on your behalf, and hope I can repair the damage to the image of the college that your irresponsible actions have caused.'

Carly opened her mouth, but then shut it again firmly—after all, she was in the wrong—and went out, just resisting the powerful impulse to slam the door behind her. Image—yes, of course, that was what was really bugging him. He didn't care a jot about the inconvenience to Bradley's, only about any possible damage to the college, and therefore to the precious person of Dr Jutson.

Arms folded, she stared across the playing fields, idly watching as the football teams drifted back to the changing-rooms, then instead focused on her own reflection in the glass. Flushed with anger and mortification—even the pale shadow of herself revealed that—her wide hazel eyes were sparking with barely contained temper, her full, generous mouth pursed tight.

Through the door floated smooth phrases. 'Do apologise...administrative mix-up. You know how it is, I'm sure, Mr Bradley...Miss Sheppard, our youngest member of staff, still rather inexperienced.' Here, the eavesdropper tossed back her shoulder-length fair hair and scowled at the door '...most upset... Yes, she is here, if you'd like to speak to her. Miss Sheppard,' he raised his voice to summon her back and held the phone out to her, 'Mr Bradley would like to speak to you.'

And Mr Bradley had been a perfect old sweetie. He'd assured her, in that blunt, down-to-earth Yorkshire accent which she'd grown to love, that the foundry would be very happy to have her, she was to do exactly as she wished while she was with them, and no, he was quite sure the misunderstanding had not been her fault.

As she hung up, with more than a twinge of guilt, the principal said suavely, 'Well, that's settled, then. You're to go in on Mondays and Tuesdays, starting next week. Mr Fenton will take over 5S in your absence, until a more permanent replacement can be found.'

He was doing it on purpose, of course. Choosing the most unsympathetic member of staff, who had one way only of dealing with would-be troublemakers—swift physical punishment. But there was no point in protesting.

'Oh, and Miss Sheppard.' She paused, her hand on the door knob. 'Mr Bradley is expecting you at seven forty-five a.m. On the dot.'

Carly gave him a sweet smile. 'Don't worry, Dr Jutson. I'll be there—seven forty-five. On the dot.'

And so she had been, coming in through the foundry gates with the workforce, and now she was still sitting here, outside Mr Bradley's office, like a fool, at—she shot back the cuff of her navy silk blouse—eight forty-seven, having only seen, in the past hour, the secretary and the snarling oaf who had stormed through five minutes ago.

And the oaf was still snarling. From through the almost closed door she heard, 'And what the hell did you want to go and get pregnant for? Tell that husband of yours I hold him personally responsible for this disaster!'

'I should just hope you do!' the secretary laughed. 'Look, Nick, you know you'll manage perfectly well without me.'

'No, I shan't,' a shade sulkily.

'Well, you'll have to, I'm afraid.'

Carly was listening with growing interest, and more than a twinge of envy. This pretty young woman was obviously a dab hand at dealing with ill-tempered oafs, an art which she personally had never managed to learn. Her far more negative response had always been to erect a set of defensive fortifications around herself and stay well inside them.

'And I suppose that one out there,' she could almost see him jerk his thumb in her direction, 'is another of the incompetent would-be replacements you're trying to foist on me. She doesn't look as though she knows one end of a word-processor from the other.'

There was an undertone murmur from the secretary, then, 'What? I don't believe it. Not that bloody school-teacher? The one who should have been here in September?'

'Yes, but there seems to have been a mix-up.' The secretary's tone was soothing.

'Well, I can't help that. She's six weeks too late. Tell her to go away.'

'No, I certainly will not!' Carly sucked in her breath in horror. 'If you don't want to see her, you can tell her yourself. Your father asked her to come in this morning——'

Father? Oh, God—that meant, didn't it, that the oaf was a Bradley too?

'Oh, so this was his idea, was it? He knows very well I didn't want to be lumbered with a prissy schoolteacher following me round——'

Following *him* round? Horrified, Carly leapt to her feet and, with a single perfunctory knock, went into the office. Both of them swung round to her, the secretary merely with a look of surprise, while the man gave her a swift, wholly masculine glance of appraisal, openly taking in the slender, rangy lines of her body, accentuated by the fluid cut of the soft wool suit, the shining shoulder-length bob of fair hair set off by the blue-green colouring of the suit, and finally her delicate oval face. Just for a split second, disconcertingly, there was a flicker as though of recognition in the dark blue eyes, although she knew they had never met before, but then it was gone.

'I'm sorry,' she began, rather self-conscious now, as the effect of her grand entrance still seemed to hang in the air, 'but there appears to be some mistake. I have an appointment with Mr James Bradley.'

'No, you don't,' he grunted sourly. 'My father never comes down to the foundry on a Monday these days. He's arranged this as a little welcome back treat for me.'

That did it. Carly, her bosom swelling with outrage, had had enough. She'd intended to make her apologies to Mr Bradley, Senior, in his absence and leave as swiftly as possible, but suddenly her temper came to the boil. She jammed her fists hard into her jacket pockets.

'Just to put the record straight, Mr Bradley, my not turning up in September was not due to any administrative breakdown. I didn't want to come here then, and now——' now that I've seen *you*, she almost added '—I want to even less.'

'In that case, there's the door. Why stay, wasting your time and mine?'

With cool deliberation he picked up one of the files from the desk and began sifting through it.

'For one reason only, I assure you,' she snapped. 'If I refuse to take part in this scheme, my principal will have me out of the college and out of a job within the term.'

'And would that be such a disaster?' His eyes raked over her again, this time with a leisured inspection which just stopped short of insolence. 'A southerner like you, you don't belong in a place like Milton.'

'Oh, don't give me that old rubbish about effete southerners, please!' Carly's gleaming bob almost bounced with temper. 'For your information: one——' she ticked off one finger '—I'm from Gloucestershire, although I suppose in your book that makes me an effete westerner; two——' she ticked off another finger '—I happen to like living in Milton; and three——' another angry jab '—I also happen to love the kids I teach and no way am I going to walk out on them. So if that means I have to endure six months of close contact with a-an ill-mannered s-swine——' in her rage, she was stammering '—well, I'll just have to endure it, won't I?'

More than half horrified by the violence of her outburst, she stopped abruptly on a little gasp and there was complete silence in the room for a moment, as he gave her a long, speculative look.

'Hmm,' he said at last. 'Close contact, you say? But can *I* endure that, do you think? That's the question.'

And as Carly, feeling as though the high moral ground had very neatly been cut from under her feet, was still trying to conjure up some sort of reply, he turned to the secretary.

'Bring some coffee, will you, please, Di? I'm parched. And if you could rustle up a cheese sandwich or something—there was no catering on the flight to Manchester.'

He shrugged himself out of his short navy cashmere coat, to reveal a rather crumpled-looking lightweight pale grey suit and white shirt. He tossed it in the direction of the coat stand—ornamental, Victorian-style cast-iron, Carly registered—and sat down at the big, untidy desk. Peremptorily, he gestured her to a chair opposite and she sank into it, grateful for its support.

Whatever had come over her? Normally, men—even the dreaded Dr Jutson—just did not get to her; she simply didn't allow them to. Hadn't her mother always said, They're not worth the hassle, none of them? Never talk back to them—just let them have their own way, and knock hell out of all the saucepans in the kitchen later.

So why had she allowed this man, whom she didn't even know, and didn't want to know, to burrow instantly under her skin and set up a reaction so violent that it made her itch to leap at him and scratch out his eyes?

Those eyes—beautiful, dark midnight-blue eyes—were watching her over the bridge of his long fingers. As she struggled to meet that inscrutable gaze calmly, at least on the surface, he seemed to come to a decision.

He stretched out his hand across the desk. 'Nick Bradley.'

'Caroline Sheppard.' Automatically, she held out her small, pale hand and saw it engulfed in his large, tanned one.

The young woman reappeared, setting down a tray with two coffees, a round of sandwiches and a plate of biscuits.

'Oh, before I forget,' she said. 'Your sister-in-law rang last week.'

He was just lifting the sandwich from the plate. 'Simone? What the devil did she want?'

'Oh, nothing much. Just to remind you that they're expecting you next weekend for Nicky's fifth birthday.'

'Oh, hell!' He clapped his hand to his brow. 'Thanks, Di. Give her a quick ring some time, will you, and assure her that of course I couldn't possibly have forgotten my only godchild's fifth birthday.'

As the door closed, Carly, clutching at a possible straw, said, 'You've got a brother?'

'Yes. Three years younger.' He took a bite of sandwich.

'Well, then,' she said quickly, before her courage could fail her, 'perhaps I could shadow him.'

He gave a short laugh. 'Sorry to disappoint you, but the firm, in case you haven't noticed, is Bradley and Son—singular. If you want to *shadow*,' he gave the word a faintly unpleasant underlining, 'Martin, you'll have to do it in a wall-to-wall pile-carpeted accountant's office in Guildford. Of course,' once more his eyes travelled over her, 'you'd probably feel more at home there than here.'

He was baiting her again, but this time she refused to snap at the fly. 'So he's got no connection with the foundry?' she asked blandly.

'Not likely. He's got far too much sense for that. No, Martin's the brains of the family.'

Oh, come on, she thought. Behind that hard-planed face, the jutting, pugnacious jaw, there lay a quick mind and an extremely shrewd intelligence, unless she was very much mistaken. 'A First in mathematics at Cambridge, followed by a stint at the Harvard Business School— that's Martin. Whereas I, Miss Sheppard, got the hell out of school at the earliest possible moment.'

He threw her a look which said, plain as words, Want to make something of it? But Carly only gave him a cool smile and said, 'Well, I expect your father was glad for you to join him in the business, anyway.'

'That's right. So, instead of plush carpeting and a roomful of fancy computer terminals, I've got this.' And his hand seemed to encompass all the grimy foundry buildings, the cobbled yard, the wrought-iron railings and gates.

'But you wouldn't swap with him, would you?' She spoke on a sudden insight, the words coming of their own volition.

He glanced at her sharply, then, 'No, I wouldn't.' Unexpectedly, he grinned, showing large, even white teeth. 'If only because I couldn't resist for more than three days at a time the irresistible urge to take my charming sister-in-law over my knee and give her a damn good hiding.'

He caught her eye and she saw, fleetingly, a gleam of malicious humour. 'She's one of those snooty, high-class bitches that I really cannot stomach.'

And his gaze strayed deliberately across Carly's silk blouse and Liberty wool suit. It wasn't the unfortunate Simone who was being got at, it was someone much closer to hand, but even so, as she clenched her hands under cover of the desk, all she allowed herself to say, with only the slightest barb in her voice, was, 'And she's a southerner, I suppose.'

'Of course.' Again she glimpsed that wicked gleam, before he went on musingly, 'Yes, she's certainly helped Martin smooth out all his rough edges. I, though, prefer to keep mine. As you'll find out, if you stay around.'

He took a swift gulp of coffee and set the cup down again, then looked across the desk at her, his piercing dark blue gaze a challenge. 'Sure you haven't changed your mind?'

Carly put her small chin defiantly in the air. 'No, I haven't.'

One thing at least, she thought suddenly—she'd know where she was with this man, so different from anyone she'd ever met before. Infuriating and with a temper on the shortest of fuses, tough and ruthless, no doubt, but also blunt and, she was somehow quite certain, completely honest. But more than that, unlike her response to so many of the men she had encountered the last few years, she sensed deep down within herself that she was actually welcoming the challenge—whether sexual or merely business, she wasn't yet sure—that he was provokingly holding out to her. Either way—and she felt the prickling excitement run through her—she had complete confidence in her ability to meet that challenge and emerge unscathed.

'Right, then.' He drained his cup—did he ever do anything slowly?—and pushing back his chair, stood up. 'If you're ready?'

He could surely see that she wasn't, that she'd only drunk half her coffee. But, as the resentment immediately began to simmer up again, she gulped down the rest of the hot liquid and, lifting her leather shoulder-bag from the floor, stood up to follow him at a slightly more leisurely pace out of the office and down the stairs.

He was waiting for her in the yard outside, with an expression on his dark face which suggested that she had kept him hanging around for minutes rather than seconds. Carly expelled a long breath.

'Look, Mr Bradley——'

'Nick, for heaven's sake.' His scowl was irritable, but even so, out here in the crisp autumn sunshine, she could see the line of black stubble along the hard-planed jaw which, transiently at least, gave him a rather endearing look. 'The only Mr Bradley at Bradley's is my father.'

'All right, then—Nick.'

Sitting in the office facing one another, they had been on a level, more or less. Now, though, although she was quite tall, she was having to look up to him, which somehow made her feel small and insecure. She stepped back a couple of paces, but then went on determinedly,

'Look, you don't want to be lumbered with me, any more than I want to be—um—teamed up with you. Well, OK, then. This shadowing scheme doesn't specify that I have to work with you. Anyone at Bradley's would do, I'm sure.'

'Sorry,' he replied brusquely. 'I pay my workforce far too well to have them wasting their time with a——' Catching her eye, he broke off, but she supplied for him,

'Prissy schoolteacher?'

The wry flicker at his mouth acknowledged her small victory, but he only shot back the cuff of his jacket and gave the slim gold wristwatch a swift glance. 'Right, we'll start with a quick tour of the works, just to put you in the picture.' He eyed her up and down once more. 'Though why the hell you've come here tarted up in a brand new, highly expensive outfit like that—this is a working foundry, you know, not a museum. Or perhaps you assumed I spend all my time sitting in the office drinking coffee.'

'I might have done,' she said, 'but I hadn't met you then, had I? And anyway,' she went on, crossing her fingers behind her back, and hoping that God—and Liberty—would forgive the lie, 'this outfit's old and not at all expensive.'

'Hmm. You could have fooled me.' But he didn't sound at all convinced. 'Do you wear this kind of thing to school?'

'Yes, as a matter of fact I do,' she responded belligerently. 'I believe in setting an example for the children, and coming to school in jeans and baggy old sweaters isn't the sort of example I mean. And anyway——' She broke off.

'Go on.'

'Well, your father—whom I'd assumed I was working with,' she reminded him, 'sounded the sort of man who'd expect to see a woman nicely dressed always.'

'Very perceptive of you. But, speaking for myself, I'd rather you were in—er—jeans and a baggy old sweater. A *very* baggy old sweater,' he amended, with an appraising glance in the direction of her full, rounded breasts that made the colour zing in her cheeks, 'if any of my men happen to be pouring white-hot metal just as you walk past.'

Something—a barely perceptible something in his voice—sent a tremor through her, so that just for a moment, in spite of her previous self-assurance, she felt an almost overpowering urge to run—now, before it was too late—out through those high wrought-iron gates, and take the consequences. But she couldn't do that. She'd run from so much in her life already—from her parents, and their brittle shell of a marriage; from her own pampered and privileged background; from any close relationship with a man—and she wasn't going to run from this one.

All that she had to do was not let him get within danger distance of her. Her defences were in position, and they'd never let her down yet—so what harm could he possibly do? None.

All the same, though, the sooner this wretched shadowing was over and done with, the sooner she'd be back full-time with her class, and Nicholas Bradley would have faded to no more than a nasty memory.

CHAPTER TWO

'RIGHT, we'll start with the raw materials.'

Nick led her to the rear of the foundry building where there was an enormous heap of coke and several huge piles of metal, some of them thickly coated with rust.

'That's pig-iron,' he gestured towards one pile, 'over there's machinery scrap—cylinder scrap, mainly—and that's steel. That's the most expensive, of course. What proportion of steel goes into the firing depends on what we're making.'

'And what are you making?' asked Carly.

'We're just finishing a rush job for outdoor furniture— pergolas, seats and so on—for an English-style park in the Middle East. And by Thursday I want to start work on the orders I've brought back from Sydney—half a dozen cast-iron bandstands.'

'You don't let the grass grow under your feet, do you?'

'Not if I can help it, no.' He gave her a cool look. 'Not that you'll find much grass growing round here.'

She followed his gaze round the barren, metal-strewn ground, then said hastily, 'Oh, I wasn't getting at you, truly I wasn't. Are those the kind of things you usually make—bandstands and pergolas, I mean?'

He shrugged. 'If people want it and it can be cast in iron, we'll make it.'

'But I thought—at least, I expected you'd be making parts for heavy industry and things like that—not fancy ornamental stuff.'

'We can do that, of course, but a couple of years back, when business was slack, I suggested to my father that we tried a line in large Victorian-style garden urns. They went a bomb, especially, for some reason which I can't possibly fathom, with all the local antique dealers,' he smiled wryly, 'and we've taken it from there, with all kinds of architectural metalwork.'

'And is most of your work overseas?'

'No, not yet, anyway. Most of what we do is for the home market. All of these new out-of-town shopping centres want their fancy lamp standards and prettified litter bins. But we're starting to make a small name for ourselves abroad, and I intend that that name will be a damn sight bigger within five years.'

And Carly, looking at that strong face and that determined jut of jaw, suddenly had little doubt that well within five years the name of Bradley and Son would be very well known indeed.

'The firm hasn't always been Bradley's, of course,' he went on.

'Oh?'

'My father's been here all his life—worked his way up from the shop floor to management—but it had been going downhill for years—ever since the war, really. And then, when they were on the point of calling in the receivers, he organised a buy-out—invested all his own savings and redundancy money, plus a massive loan from the bank.

'That was fifteen years ago——' about the time, she thought involuntarily, that Nick had 'got the hell out of school' and joined his father here '—and it was a devil of a gamble. In fact, no one but a pig-headed fool like him——' but Carly could sense the pride in his voice '—would ever have taken it on. It's been tough going ever since, but maybe at last there's an upswing in sight. At least, he's relaxed enough now to leave most of the day-to-day running to me—although really he lost most of his drive last year, when my mother died.'

His lips tightened momentarily. 'Anyway, let's get on.'

He strode across the rough ground and down a rickety iron staircase, then pulled back a sliding door. Instantly the noise rushed out to meet them: the clanging of machines, men hammering—metal on metal—and shouting to one another, clanking chains and, above everything else, at a rate of decibels which made Carly's brain reel, piped pop music. Instinctively, her hands went up to her ears, but then, catching the sardonic gleam in Nick's eyes, she lowered them.

'Oh, one thing.' Although they were still in the doorway, he had to bring his mouth close to her ear, so that she could feel his warm breath on her cheek. 'You're insured, I presume? I certainly won't take responsibility for you otherwise.'

'You don't have to.' She too had to speak much louder than usual, so her cool tone was probably wasted on him. 'I'm here on school business, so I'm covered by the Local Authority.'

'That's all right, then. I'd hate anything to happen to you.' But he didn't look as if he would.

With the need to make themselves heard, he was standing very near her, well within the invisible male-exclusion zone she carried round with her. Their bodies were very close, their hips almost brushing, and their faces just a hand's width apart, so near that she could see herself reflected in the black pupils of those wonderful inky blue eyes, and almost count the individual black lashes that fringed them. Eyes to drown in...

She took an involuntary step back and came up painfully against a large wooden packing case.

'Watch your step,' Nick said blandly, but from the fleeting expression in those eyes Carly was quite sure that he knew exactly why she'd made that small, almost timorous movement.

On a rack beside the door were several battered-looking hard hats. He lifted one down, blew away a film of black dust from its rim and handed it to her. 'Put this on.'

And Carly, thinking with resignation of her newly washed hair, suppressed a little grimace of distaste as her fingers came into contact with its gritty surface and perched it daintily on top of her head.

'I said put it on, for God's sake!' Nick shook his head impatiently and, before she could move back out of range, jammed it down hard over her ears, then turned and led the way along the first aisle.

Underfoot everywhere was a thick layer of fine black sand; Carly's heels sank into it as she tried to keep up with him. Why on earth had she worn these shoes, beige kid leather with slim heels? she asked herself in silent exasperation. Because she'd been intent on impressing Bradley Senior, that was why.

A group of men were working at a low, stationary conveyor belt, pouring sand into large metal moulds, patting it down, levelling it. They were engrossed in their work but looked up briefly, nodding at Nick and giving Carly a swift, curious glance.

'Most of the moulds we use are sand.' Nick's voice in her ear again, this time so close that his lips brushed against her—just once, but her skin tingled uncomfortably for minutes afterwards. 'But if it's a one-off casting we use polystyrene.'

He pointed to where, further along the conveyor belt, a large white form was being manoeuvred into position.

'Polystyrene? How on earth does it withstand the molten iron?'

'It doesn't,' he replied briefly. 'It vaporises—disappears into thin air. But it holds its shape just long enough for the iron cast to form.'

'And what's it going to be?' That incongruous, light-as-air mould intrigued her. In fact, in spite of the hostility she still felt for this place—and the man so uncomfortably close beside her—she found herself becoming increasingly fascinated by the foundry, so different from any place she'd ever seen before, almost another world.

'It's a part of the clock for the new pedestrianised precinct in Milton. That's a real one-off, although you never know, it may lead to similar orders.'

He led the way across to the far side of the foundry where two gigantic brick floor-to-roof cones stood side by side.

'These are our blast furnaces. We use them alternately—one's out of use each day being relined.'

The doors of the shut-down furnace were open and, peering inside, Carly could see two men plastering the walls with wet clay.

'Why do you have to do that every time?' she asked.

'Because the iron melts at over fourteen hundred degrees Centigrade,' he said laconically.

'How long does it take to get the furnace to that temperature?'

'Oh, about two hours. If we're in a hurry, though——' which, of course, you never are, she thought '—we stuff it with rags soaked in diesel oil and then——' he flashed her a sudden, boyish grin '—we stand back.'

He turned away for a moment to speak to a man who was adjusting the powerful blue gas jet which was directed into the heart of the other furnace.

Heavens, it was hot here—even hotter than in the other parts of the building—with that roaring jet of gas just beside her. Carly flexed her shoulders uncomfortably and felt a trickle of sweat run down her neck. Under the rigid hat, her hair was beginning to stick to her forehead and nape.

She shot Nick a resentful look. No one else was wearing a helmet—it was just him being difficult with her. Surreptitiously, she eased it back, then, when he did not seem to notice, took it off completely, drawing the back of her arm across her clammy forehead with a sigh of relief.

'Put that back on!'

Nick's face, dark with anger, was turned to her and in the same second she saw out of the corner of her eye a metal container, shaped like a huge ladle and suspended from an overhead conveyor belt, bearing down on her. It was way above her head, but even so she hastily jammed on her hat and stepped back a couple of paces—and felt one heel go down heavily into a shallow pit of sooty black water.

Ugh! She glanced up, but then, catching the glint of grim satisfaction in Nick's eyes, suppressed her grimace of disgust and merely drew out her foot, black-streaked and dripping past the ankle. He beckoned her peremptorily towards him, but Carly, her lips tightening, pretended not to notice. But then, as he took a step towards her, she saw the anger in his eyes again and reluctantly squelched her way across.

'I was explaining to Joe what you're doing here,' he said brusquely, 'and he's keen to meet you.'

Unlike some people I could mention, she thought caustically even as she found herself returning the warm smile of the man who had been working the gas jet.

'Caroline Sheppard—this is Joe Stephens. Joe's been with us—what is it?—thirty years now. He's our furnaceman.'

The man, grey-haired and with a deeply lined face, rubbed his hand against his boiler suit and held it out.

'Pleased to meet you, Miss Sheppard. I've heard a lot about you from our Douggie.'

'Douggie?' Light dawned. 'Oh, you mean Douggie Stephens.'

'Yes, that's right. I'm his grandad.'

'I'm very pleased to meet you, Mr Stephens.' She took his hand, giving him a wide smile. 'Douggie's a great lad—I'm really fond of him.'

He pulled a face. 'You're the first teacher to say that, I'm sure, miss.'

'Oh well, I know he has his off days, but his heart's in the right place. Please tell his parents he's coming on well. I'm very——'

'Oh, but miss, he lost his mum two years back.'

The man's face clouded as Carly stared at him, horrified by her blunder. The new principal refused to reveal the pupils' individual records, so unless they chose to be communicative she was quite unaware of their backgrounds. Impulsively, she took his hand.

'I'm so sorry, Mr Stephens.'

'Well, these things happen. But his dad was really worried about Douggie a while back—he took it very hard. Since you've had him, though, he's been a new lad.' He gave her a quick grin. 'He'd kill me for saying so, but he really thinks the world of you—they all do. You've got a rare gift with those kids, my lass—got them all eating out of your hand.'

Carly coloured with pleasure at the unexpected compliment, then, past his shoulder, caught Nick's glance. He had been standing to one side, a silent observer, and now she glimpsed, for the first time in their brief acquaintance, a gleam of something that looked almost like respect.

She returned the other man's smile. 'Well, I think it's just that I love them all,' she said simply.

'And I'll tell Jim what you said about our lad. Now,' he turned to Nick, 'I think we're about ready.'

Nick nodded and, as the furnaceman gestured a couple of hands across, he lifted down a heavy padded coat from a nail in the wall and got into it, as did the other three, then they all put on helmets complete with reinforced plastic face-masks.

Carly thought that he'd forgotten about her, but then he came towards her carrying a spare visor.

'Keep still,' he said as she drew back, and she obeyed, allowing him to snap the shield into place on her hard hat.

'Are you going to empty the furnace?' she asked.

He paused, his hands still adjusting the fastening, and looked down, taking in her flushed face, then nodded. 'Why?'

'It's really exciting.' Spontaneously, she smiled up at him, her eyes sparkling. 'All that red-gold molten metal.'

'Sorry to disappoint you,' he said mechanically, as though most of his mind was on something else, 'but a good firing isn't red, it's white—near enough the colour of an electric light filament.'

'Oh. But anyway, all those showers of sparks and so on.'

'It's molten steel that makes those, not iron,' Nick said briefly, but she wasn't going to let him dampen her spirits.

'Well, I know you see it every day, but I'm sure I'll find it exciting, anyway,' she said firmly, and took a step towards the other three men, who were sliding the metal ladle into place at the end of the channel which ran from the furnace base.

He caught her arm roughly. 'Where the hell do you think you're going?'

'To watch, of course.'

'Well, you're not watching from here.' And as she tried to protest, he towed her right across to the back wall. 'Stay there.'

'Oh, but I shan't——'

'No buts. If you move a muscle, out you go. All right?'

Oh, yes, sir, no, sir, three bags full, sir. 'All right,' she muttered.

'Good.' He gave her a look that showed that he knew exactly what she'd been thinking then, snapping down his visor, walked away.

One of the men held out a pair of heavy gloves; Nick put them on and the four of them gathered round the furnace door. Joe knocked away a plug at the top of the channel and within seconds, not roaring, as her imagination had expected, but with no more than an angry hiss, a steady stream of pure white liquid fire came trickling down the channel and into the ladle.

So he'd got his good firing. At the thought of Nick, Carly's eyes swivelled to him. Through the grimy visor, the four men, all dressed in those bulky, anonymous coats, looked the same, yet somehow she picked him out. This end of the foundry was dark, but the incandescent brilliance of the metal lit the front of the furnace like a stage set and, silhouetted against it in stark black relief, his figure looked even larger, more menacing.

His back was towards her, but then he swung round and through the visor his face glistened with sweat— even where she was standing, she could feel the very ends of the blast waves of heat coming off the furnace—and she saw his expression, a combination of fierce concentration and exhilaration. There was a small eruption of sparks, which reflected back from his visor, giving him for a moment an unearthly look, almost like Lucifer himself at the gates of hell; then he turned away again.

The first ladle was filled and carried away on the moving belt towards the men who were waiting at the other end of the foundry to pour the metal into the moulds, and another was swung into position, filled, then another. At last, that brilliant light died away, the men pulled off their gloves and coats, raised their face masks to mop their brows, and Nick was coming towards her.

'That was marvellous!' Still held by the excitement which had gripped her, she could barely wait for him to get within speaking range.

He looked down at her for a moment without replying, a rather enigmatic expression on his face, then asked at last, 'Even without the sparks?'

'Yes, even without the sparks. It was a good one, wasn't it?'

'Yes, it was.'

He reached across to snap off her visor before pulling her helmet away. As he did so, his fingers brushed against her face and lifted a few strands of hair from her forehead. Tensing with this sudden, unexpected body contact, they stared at one another for the endless span of one heartbeat, then Nick said abruptly, 'Time for the meeting.'

And without looking to see if she was following him, he strode off past the furnace, which was still giving off waves of heat, through the side door and out into the yard.

'That's settled, then. Giles,' Nick glanced at the be-spectacled young man who had been introduced to Carly as the company's pattern-maker, and who had spent the first few minutes of the meeting surreptitiously ogling her until he'd caught Nick's steely eye, after which he'd resolutely looked anywhere but at her. 'You'll have the designs ready by Wednesday. And Ray——' a nod in the direction of the foundry manager '—we'll gear the production line for this from Thursday.'

Shooting back his cuff, he looked at his watch. 'Right. Lunch.'

As he leaned forward to gather up the papers which lay scattered across the table, Carly saw the two men exchange a silent grimace. For the last hour and a half she had been sitting rather self-consciously alongside him—when they'd first entered his office she'd made for a seat in the furthest corner, but Nick had rather irritably waved her to the chair at his right elbow—but now she stood up, picked up her bag and made to follow them out.

'Just a moment, Miss Sheppard.' Nick's voice held her in the doorway, so she waited while he rammed the papers into his briefcase, put on his jacket, then preceded her down the stairs and out into the yard once more.

As they emerged, a hooter sounded and Carly, confidently expecting to be ungraciously dismissed for the lunch break, was already turning away.

'Where do you think you're going?' A large hand, its touch warm and solid through the thin wool of her suit, closed over her elbow.

'To my car, to get——'

'This way.'

He was already guiding her unwilling feet, not in the direction of her pale blue Mini Special but towards a sleek red Aston Martin. As she stared blankly at him, he opened the passenger side.

'Get in,' he ordered.

'But why?'

'Lunch,' he replied succinctly.

'Oh—no, really.' Horrified, Carly shrank back, clutching her shoulder bag for support. 'I—I've brought my lunch. It's in my car—over there.'

'In,' he repeated, with a little shove at her back, and, because she had the distinct impression that if she prevaricated a moment longer he would pick her up and, under the interested gaze of the bunch of workmen who were emerging at the far end of the yard, dump her inside, she scrambled into the bucket seat.

As he slid in beside her, she had one final try. 'But I don't really bother with a proper meal at lunchtime.'

'Well, *I* do,' he grunted, and reversed out of the parking space at a speed which made her toes curl in terror. 'And if you're supposed to be shadowing me for the day—well, you come too.'

'Isn't there a works canteen?' she asked as he swept out through the gates.

'Of course, but we're not eating there. And yes, it's perfectly good enough for me, usually, just in case you think I'm above such things,' he shot her a sideways look, 'but not today.'

'Look.' Carly cleared her throat and went on determinedly, 'I'm sure this shadowing arrangement doesn't really mean lunchtimes as well, and it certainly doesn't mean that you have to buy me lunch, if that's what you're intending. In fact, I'd far rather you didn't,' she added rather stiffly, as Nick, all his attention apparently on the narrow, congested road ahead, gave no sign of having heard her protests.

She gave his hard profile a quick glance, then, seeing that there was absolutely no response forthcoming, turned her head away to stare out at the small, neat villas which they were passing. She felt cross and dispirited;

throughout the long morning she had been looking forward to at least an hour's respite from this abrasive whirlwind of a man, who was already beginning to exhaust her by his sheer physical energy, before what she was quite sure would be an equally long afternoon. Now, though, she was being denied even that concession.

They were on the outskirts of Milton now, at the opposite end of town from her own cottage and the college; she'd never been here before and she looked about her with interest. He turned down a side road, lined with large Edwardian houses set in their own grounds, then a few hundred yards further on swung into a narrow, steeply raked lane, before finally turning off into a driveway fringed with tall laurels and rhododendrons, which opened at last to lawns and a large house.

He parked at the foot of the steps with a spurt of gravel from the rear wheels, got out, slammed his door and came round to her side. This must be the Milton Country Club. She'd heard of it, of course—the restaurant's reputation was renowned throughout the county. In spite of what he'd said, he was just showing off—he wasn't even lowering himself to drive round to the car park, which was presumably at the rear of the building. Or, at the very least, he was trying to throw her off balance, and she had to start in the way she meant to go on.

As he opened the door, she sat tight. 'Now let's just get this straight,' she began, in her best 5S tone.

'Yes, Teach?' he responded instantly, raising his black brows enquiringly.

'And don't call me that!' She tapped her foot irritably against the carpet. 'I've already told you that I don't want you to buy me lunch, but if you do, I insist on buying yours tomorrow.'

'You do?'

'Yes, and then we'll be quits. I don't want any favours from you.'

'Shut up,' he said briefly.

'I beg your pardon?'

'I said, shut up.' He scowled down unamiably at her, but she was *not* going to be intimidated by this bully.

'No, I won't, and I won't get out of the car until you agree to—ow! Let go of me!'

And next moment, with no clear idea of how she had got there, she was standing on the gravel beside him, a reddening patch on one wrist.

'You'll soon learn, I'm sure, Miss Sheppard, that I like my women to do as they're told.'

'I'm quite sure you do, but you see, I'm——'

'Incessant argument over every trivial request annoys me, I'm afraid.'

'Well, is that so?' Carly, hands on hips, tossed back her silky fair hair and returned his scowl. 'Let me tell you one thing, *Mr* Bradley. I am *not* your woman. That is a fact which I am extremely glad about. And I would also like to say that I feel *extremely* sorry for any unfortunate woman who is. Your woman,' she added, in case any of the sense of her garbled sentence had been lost on him.

'Oh, but you are, my dear Miss Sheppard,' he purred. 'Of course, I don't know which brave man you belong to from Wednesday to Sunday each week, but for the next five months, on Mondays and Tuesdays, you belong to me. And I've suddenly realised that that may have its uses, after all.'

'W-what do you mean by that?' There was an expression in those dark blue eyes which she did not at all care for.

'You'll see. Oh, by the way,' he went on, apparently at a tangent, 'you remember that phone call I took just as we were leaving?'

'Yes?'

'I forgot to mention, it was from your esteemed Dr Jutson.'

'What did he want?' she asked.

'Oh, just a polite enquiry—he does sound such a nice man, by the way—to make sure you were settling down all right. Mind you, I got the distinct impression that what he was really doing was making sure that you'd turned up at all.'

As Carly's lips tightened, he continued smoothly, 'I'd hate to have to ring him back this afternoon and tell him that you were proving stubborn and uncooperative and that I think that for all concerned it would be better to call the whole thing off.'

And with that he went round to the car boot, lifted out a large black leather case and mounted the steps, leaving her to trail mutinously after him. Reaching into his pocket, he brought out a key ring and unlocked the door, then turned and caught her expression.

'Yes, that's right. This is my house.'

Of course, she should have known. Square and solid, built in the local millstone grit which gave it a bleakly uncompromising look—as uncompromising as its owner. He saw her glance up at the façade.

'A Victorian ironmaster's residence—I bought it a couple of years ago. Very fitting, don't you think?' He gave her a mocking smile and threw open the door. 'Come into my parlour.'

The entrance hall was large and impressive, with beautiful old oak panelling and a wide sweep of staircase, also in oak, which led up towards a galleried landing. From here, a huge Victorian stained glass window, with a pre-Raphaelite knight and his lady in a lush grove of almost tropical foliage, spilled tiny jewelled pools of light down the stair-treads and across the parquet floor at their feet.

'Oh, it's beautiful!' Carly, her face raised upwards, clasped her hands in spontaneous pleasure.

'Yes, it is, isn't it?'

She turned, to see him regarding not the window, but her and felt, beneath the dazzling glow of amber, jade, rose and turquoise on her skin, a slow blush start. He was standing so near her that she could feel the warmth from him, smell that faint yet disturbing scent of male body and sweat.

'But surely you're aware,' he set the case down at the foot of the staircase, 'that even ironmasters have souls, Miss Sheppard.'

'Oh, for heaven's sake!' The knowledge that she was on his territory, the realisation of the effect that his nearness was having on her, made her scratchy. 'Call me Carly. Everybody does.'

'Carly.' He said the name over in his deep voice, then, 'Come on through to the kitchen.'

'No—wait. I must do something about my feet—look.' He glanced down as she held up for his inspection one slim ankle, smeared with black puddle water, and a once-beige shoe. 'It'll only take me a couple of minutes,' she said, then added sweetly, 'I'm sure even you can spare that much from your busy schedule.'

He frowned consideringly, so that she thought he was going to insist that he couldn't, but then led the way down a corridor, dark after the brilliant glow from that window, and pushed open a door.

'I trust this will do.' Faint irony underscored his tone. 'Unless, of course, you feel you need a full-scale bath.'

Carly surveyed the opulent cloakroom, with its fittings of pretty hand-painted Victorian-style ceramics and matching tiles.

'Thank you, this will be fine,' she said formally, as though she were a guest reassuring a hotelier who was inviting her to inspect her room, then stood clutching her bag until she heard his footsteps going back down the corridor.

She slid the bolt firmly, then perched on the lavatory pedestal which, like the handbasin, was wreathed in twining white convolvulus and pink and white rosebuds. Easing herself out of her shoes, which were full of grit, she peeled off her tights, wrinkling her nose with distaste.

It seemed almost sacrilege to bring the convolvulus and rosebuds of the basin into contact with the filthy nylon, but she swilled them through, before hurriedly washing each foot in turn and dabbing it dry on the pink towel. Then, clutching her tights in a damp ball, she opened the door.

Her host was lounging in the doorway of a room further along the corridor; when she appeared, he glanced pointedly at his watch, but without a word gestured her past. Putting her nose in the air, Carly stalked past him and found herself in a huge square kitchen, lined with super-modern bleached wood units, along with fridge, freezer and dishwasher.

'What a lovely room!' It came out in spite of her resolution to say not a word, and she thought almost enviously of the small neat kitchen-diner in her cottage, where every inch of space had to count. 'Did you install it when you moved in?'

Next to dignified silence, trivial conversation, she'd now decided, was going to be the best way of getting through this enforced intimacy—not only this lunchtime, but every Monday and Tuesday between now and Easter.

'Yes. When I bought Fellside, there was an old cooker and cracked sink over there, a few cupboards—oh, and plenty of rats. Don't worry, though,' he added as she glanced nervously around her, 'they're gone.'

At that moment, her stomach gave a long, anguished rumble. 'Oops! Sorry.' She clutched it, laughing rather self-consciously.

Nick regarded her sternly. 'Did you have any breakfast?'

'Well——' she pulled a face '—to be honest, I was too keen to make sure that I wasn't late on my first morning to bother with much.'

'Hmm. Well, in that case, you'd better get started.'

Carly looked round her hopefully, but there was no sign of food, no place settings for two laid out neatly on the big square table in the middle of the room.

'I'm going to shower.' Nick was already loosening his tie. 'I haven't had one since Sydney.' He grimaced. 'Don't tell me—not before time. So I'll leave you to get on with it, then.'

She stared at him across the table, open-mouthed. 'You mean,' her voice was strangled, 'you've dragged me all the way up here just to cook your lunch?'

CHAPTER THREE

'OF COURSE,' Nick replied, matter-of-factly. 'Yours too, of course. The larder's through there. Help yourself to anything you fancy—whatever you want to get is all right by me.'

'Well, of all the——' Suddenly, all the pent-up irritation and resentment which had been simmering since early that morning came to a head and boiled over. 'You've got some nerve—you know that, Nick Bradley?'

'If you say so,' he responded coolly. 'Are you going to prepare this meal or aren't you?'

'I'm damned if I will! Skivvying for you isn't part of our arrangement and you know it. Cook your own lunch.'

'Look,' he began, clearly reining in his own temper with an effort, 'I've got an important meeting this afternoon starting in not much more than an hour. I want to shower and shave.' He ran his fingers across his chin. 'You may fancy me with my macho whiskers——'

'Fancy you?' Carly spluttered. 'Of all the——'

'But my colleagues at the Chamber of Commerce,' he continued smoothly, 'prefer me a little sleeker. I've eaten very little all day—in fact, I've had one hell of a twenty-four hours—and as Mrs Preston, my housekeeper, is away until tonight, it seemed an excellent idea to take advantage of your charming presence.'

Carly toyed irresolutely with the neckline of her suit. Perhaps he wasn't being so unreasonable, after all. If only he hadn't seemed to be taking her so much for granted, or at least had a more graceful way of putting things—like, just for once in his life, saying 'please', for instance—she'd have been delighted to cook his wretched lunch for him. Maybe if she pointed this out to him, gave him the chance to see the error of his ways and reform...

'Well, all right,' she conceded. 'I suppose I could——'

'Don't bother to lay on anything elaborate—we haven't got time.'

All Carly's good intentions evaporated like snow in the sunshine.

'Oh, dear, what a pity! And I was planning on providing a five-star cordon bleu spread.'

'Ah, well. I look forward to that another time.'

'Another time?' She almost spluttered with indignation. 'You've just got to be joking. I promise you, this is the first and last meal I get for you—ever!'

They were glowering across the table at each other, like a pair of fighting cocks, when all at once Nick expelled a long breath.

'I've told you already, I've had a hairy time—very little sleep, very little food—so be a good girl and humour me—just this once, of course.' And suddenly he flashed her another of those totally disarming grins. 'You make a start, and I'll give you a hand when I've had my shower.'

As he half turned away, Carly said, 'Are you quite sure you don't want me to follow you in there and scrub your back, oh, lord and master?' Too late, the words out, she caught herself up with a little gasp.

'Well now, Carly——' he turned back to give her a long look '—I would say that's entirely up to you.'

She stared at him, all her anger on the instant turning against herself, so that she could have bitten her runaway tongue off at the root. She never allowed herself to indulge in pert sexual backchat—she'd never even wanted to, had always kept well out of any such verbal sparring in the college staff-room. She much preferred to keep safely under cover behind her defensive wall—and now here she was, her rashness leaving her exposed in open ground.

'You know,' she said tightly, 'I just wonder what Councillor Farnell—the chairman of the Education Committee—would say if he saw me here.'

Nick paused in the doorway just long enough to slant her a wicked smile. 'Jim? Oh, I'm sure he'd be quite happy. No doubt, like any good Yorkshireman, he believes that a woman's place is definitely in the kitchen.' Then, just as he was closing the door, he added, 'That's if she isn't in the bedroom, of course.' And he had gone.

Carly stared at the door panels, feeling the last residue of temper ooze away. Well, you asked for that, didn't you? she thought savagely. You really set yourself up. It wasn't him, of course—it was her own reaction which had got the better of her. How many times do I have to tell you? she ranted silently. Don't react, and he can't touch you. In future, she would keep such a hold on herself that nothing—absolutely nothing—would get through...

In the meantime, though, he would doubtless be back in record time, demanding his meal. Realising that she was still clutching her tights, she went across to the large gas boiler in the far corner, let down the hoist above it with a tug which all but made it leap from its runners, and laid them over it, then drew it up again with a final vicious jerk.

Snatching down a navy and white butcher's apron which hung from a peg by the door, she put it on and went to inspect the contents of the fridge and freezer. Well, there was plenty to choose from—everything from smoked salmon to T-bone steaks. Obviously her host believed in keeping that large frame amply supplied with food. But something quick was what she needed...

Beside the fridge was a tray of free-range eggs from the local farm where she bought her own, and when she went into the larder, among all the tinned food, she found several of baby mushrooms. Opening two tins, she drained them, then began slicing the harmless contents on the chopping board as though she were sawing through someone's jugular.

While they gently sautéd in a little hot butter and oil on the split-level cooker, she broke half a dozen of the eggs into a basin, then rinsed some of the large beef tomatoes, lettuce, endive and watercress she found in the crisper. Finally she fetched some of the bread rolls which she had seen in the freezer and slid them in the oven to warm through.

Her tights, a fine fifteen denier, were almost dry when she felt the toes. Maybe she ought to get into them now; if she knew Nick Bradley—and she was beginning to think that, unfortunately, she did—she'd be back in the car before she had time to get more than a dozen mouthfuls of lunch inside her.

She dragged them down off the hoist and, perching awkwardly against the kitchen table, rolled up one leg and thrust her big toe into it. What an arrogant, overbearing swine he is, she thought moodily... However am I going to bear the next five months? It's a life sentence... So help me, before I'm through, I'll——

'Now, how can I help?'

The voice, a few inches behind her, made her almost leap clear through her skin. She lost her balance, lurched against the table and would have fallen if he had not seized hold of her by the waist. Shaking herself free from his strong grip, she swung round.

'I wish——' she began, then stopped dead.

He had shaved, and showered—his hair, still barely dry, lay close around his face in damp black curls—and he had changed. He was now wearing more formal dark grey trousers, which hugged his flat abdomen and strong, narrow flanks in a clinging embrace, and a clean white shirt, open at the neck, which with his dark curls gave him a foreign, almost gypsyish air. While in the foreground of her mind she was taking all this in, something—a half-formulated thought—was tugging for recognition, but she had no time to puzzle it out.

'You wish——?'

Nick, all solicitude, prompted her and, realising that one half of the tights was still flapping around her ankle, Carly made a huge effort to pull herself together.

'I wish you wouldn't sneak up on me like that.'

He'd caught her off balance in more ways than one, but, trying to summon all her poise, she went on coolly, 'If you want, you can prepare the salad.' And without quite looking at him she pushed the wooden bowl across the table.

'Right.'

As he turned away, throwing his jacket and tie, which had been slung from one hand, across the nearest chair, she frantically pulled up her tights under cover of the butcher's apron, in her haste pushing her thumb right through the fine silky knit. Bang goes one pair of Christian Dior tights, she thought sourly, and, turning to the unit, began arranging cheeses on a plate.

Nick seemed at once totally absorbed in his task; Carly, on the other hand, was only aware of his presence. She felt her eyes drift sideways towards him of their own volition as he took up a sharp chef's knife and began work. Fascinated, she watched those strong, capable fingers as he swiftly sliced the tomatoes and arranged

them in a pottery dish. For all that she was quite certain
that the owner of those fingers was perfectly able to
undertake any of the heavy jobs in the foundry, they
seemed to reveal a surprising sensitivity. There, perhaps,
lay the clue to this man's complex personality: a man
who could dexterously manoeuvre molten metal into a
mould, yet gain sensuous pleasure from owning a house
with a beautiful stained glass window in it.

Those fingers—strong, brown, warm. Hadn't she already felt their warmth? They were surely lover's fingers,
weren't they? An image suddenly came into her mind of
those fingers, making skilled love to the woman beside
him—roving over her body, making her give up her
secrets to him, and drawing from her wild, unthinking
responses, which she had not known herself capable
of——

Carly, struggling to free herself from those smothering
images that gripped her, took a deep breath and forced
all her attention back to the cheeses.

'Damn!' She turned to see Nick frowning, the wooden
spoon and fork with which he had been dressing the salad
suspended over the bowl. 'I forgot the wine.'

'Oh, don't bother. I never drink at——' she began,
but he had already snatched a key from a nail beside the
door and disappeared along the passage, returning a
couple of minutes later with a bottle of red wine.

He uncorked it and stood it on the central heating
boiler, then turned to her with a rueful smile. 'What an
appalling way to treat a St Julien, but we haven't got
time to sit around waiting for it to come up to room
temperature—it's pretty cold down in the cellar.'

'You've got a proper wine cellar?'

'Yes, a huge one. After I'd bought this place, I found
whole cases of old wine down there. I had happy visions
of knocking back a magnum of Bollinger '29 every night

for months.' Over his shoulder, he gave her a quick, engaging smile, which she simply had to respond to. 'In the event, though, they all turned out to taste of vinegar—or worse.'

As he came back to the table, Carly, her eyes fixed on the cheese board and a wicker bowl of apples and grapes she was carrying, stepped back and they collided sharply, sending several of the apples flying.

'Oh, sorry, my fault,' she exclaimed, as he bent to return them.

'Tell me, are you going to make a habit of this? First my precious files, now these?' Nick enquired, as he dropped them into the bowl.

But then, as he did so, he looked down full at her. Just for a moment there was that flicker which she had seen in his eyes when they'd first met, and *something*—she couldn't say what—seemed to flare in the air between them, leaving her heart beating in irregular bounding leaps and her breath almost wrenched out of her as though, just for that infinitesimal moment, that something had sent her whirling up into the air, then set her down again on the tiled floor, not a hair out of place.

'Th-thank you,' she murmured confusedly, as he took the cheese and fruit from her limp hand and put them down on the table. 'I—I must make the omelette.'

Catching up the bowl of eggs, she gratefully turned her back on him and set to work. With every nerve heightened, though, she was conscious all the time of his presence as he moved around the kitchen, opening cupboards, setting out glasses, lifting down a coffee percolator and filling it...

'More wine?' Nick held out the bottle, his words breaking the constrained silence that had fallen on them for the last few minutes, but Carly shook her head firmly.

'No, thank you.'

'Very wise.' He gave her a slightly mocking smile as he half filled his own glass. 'But I think I'll have a little more, if only to dull the boredom of the meeting this afternoon.'

With infinite care, she spread butter on to a water biscuit, then cut a small piece of Wensleydale and ate it slowly, letting the tangy cheese melt in her mouth. Then, as she finished it, she glanced up covertly from under the screen of her lashes at the man sitting opposite her. But he was already watching her and, caught out, her pulses once again leaping with guilty confusion, she hurriedly pushed back her chair.

'I-I'll clear away.' She dared not look at him this time.

'No.' He put out his hand to restrain her. 'I'll do that. Go on through to the sitting-room—it's at the end of the corridor—and I'll bring the coffee. Oh, and Carly——' She hesitated, turning slowly in the doorway. 'Thanks for the meal.'

'That's all right,' she said, a shade awkwardly. 'I'm—well, sorry if I overreacted a bit.'

'Well,' he pulled a wry face, 'I wasn't exactly at my sunny best myself. So let's call it—what was it?—quits, shall we?'

The sitting-room was a large, high-ceilinged room, pleasantly furnished with a comfortable-looking suite, loose-covered with Sanderson golden lily fabric, arranged round a huge stone fireplace which held a cast-iron wood-burning stove. The carpet was a soft, neutral green, which set off the pieces of antique oak furniture, the two large copper jugs of white chrysanthemums and the landscape oil paintings.

Somehow Carly found it difficult to picture Nick sprawled at his ease here—so tranquil a room for such a turbulent, larger-than-life character. And yet, she thought involuntarily, maybe it matched an inner calm—or certainly an inner strength, that she already sensed in him.

In one corner was a CD player and a rack of discs, but Carly headed straight for the bookcase which took up the entire width of one wall. Raymond Chandler, P.D. James, Dickens, Mrs Gaskell, the Brontës stood alongside books on potholing and the Industrial Revolution. Did all this, too, tell her something about the man?

'Want to borrow any?'

Nick's voice came from behind her and she started, colouring slightly.

'Sorry—I was being nosy. I can't resist other people's books—their taste intrigues me.'

He set down the tray on a side table. 'And what does your inspection of my shelves tell you about me?' As she hesitated, he added, with a faintly provocative smile, 'Do tell me.'

'Well,' she was still floundering slightly, 'you've got very wide interests. Do you really go potholing?'

'When I can—not as much as I used to, though. Have you tried it?'

'Oh, no.' She shivered. 'Go down those wet, dark holes in the ground? Ugh!'

'Oh, it's great, once you've made your first dive. I must take you some time.'

'No—no, thank you.' She shuddered again and turned back to the books. 'You like detective stories and——' she took one volume from the shelves and opened it carefully, brushing her fingers reverently over the title pages '—you're very wealthy.'

'And what makes you think that?'

'Well—this Dickens. It's a first edition, isn't it? Oh, and,' she gave him an impish grin, 'you're a true Yorkshireman—all the Brontë works.'

'Do you like them?' he asked.

'The Brontës? Oh, yes, I love them. I chose them as a special study when I was at college.'

'You've been to Haworth, to the Parsonage, then?'

'No, I'm ashamed to say I haven't.' Her face clouded. 'When I got this job I promised myself I'd go there on my very first weekend, but somehow, when you start teaching, there's a lot of preparation and I used to spend every weekend on it. In fact, I often still do.'

'Hmm.' He was regarding her, his lips slightly pursed. 'You shouldn't overdo it, you know. You're too young to wrap yourself up entirely in your work.'

Carly bridled slightly. 'But I love teaching—and I love my pupils, so it's no hardship, I promise you. And anyway, what about you? You're a workaholic, if ever I saw one.'

'Well, I've had to be, to turn the company round the last few years. Times haven't been easy for my line of business, you know.'

'Yes, I can imagine,' she said seriously, 'but anyway, how old are *you*?'

'Thirty-four.'

'Well then, you're far too young to wrap yourself up in your work as well.'

She smiled triumphantly up at him, but then, conscious all at once of his nearness again, she turned away to the tall french window to look out over the sweeping lawn, bounded by herbaceous borders—mostly bare now—and shrubs.

'There's not much colour at this time of year.' He had silently moved up beside her.

'No, but that *acer griseum*,' she gestured towards the maple, with its flame-red autumn colouring, 'that's really lovely still. There's one just like that in——'

She broke off abruptly. She'd been about to say, in my parents' garden—which was even more extensive than the one stretching before her—but all at once she felt reluctant to mention her parents to Nick, and fortunately he did not seem to notice.

'Do you enjoy gardening?' he asked.

They were circling one another—she sensed that—like a couple of wary animals, weighing each other up, yet covering this probing with seemingly meaningless small talk.

'Well, I do,' she replied, still playing the game, 'but the garden at my cottage is very tiny.'

He glanced down at his watch. 'There isn't time to show you round the grounds now, but let's have our coffee through here.'

Picking up the tray again, he led her to the end of the long room, where there was a pair of wide sliding doors in frosted glass.

'Now, close your eyes,' he ordered.

'Why?' She was instantly suspicious.

'Never mind. Just do as you're told.'

She heard him slide back the doors, then felt him put one hand in the small of her back, gently pushing her forward.

'Now—open them.'

And Carly could only stare, her eyes growing round with utter astonishment. They were standing in a huge conservatory, surrounded by all the warmth and scents of a tropical forest. Potted palms stood in white Versailles tubs all round the edges of the room, with flowering shrubs—scarlet abutilon, hibiscus and stephanotis—between them. Climbers rampaged luxuriantly up the walls and hung in festoons from the high, glass-domed ceiling: blue plumbago, and jasmine, from which a cloud of tiny white flower-heads drifted down to the black and white marble-tiled floor.

'You made all this?' Carly could barely speak.

Nick grinned, relishing her reaction. 'Yes—all this. I really intended it as a kind of advertisement. We'd just begun producing cast-iron Victorian-style conservatories when I moved in here, and as I couldn't get good enough publicity material I thought I'd build my own.' He indicated a group of padded loungers at one side. 'Now, I find I come in here if I've got a problem at work. It's amazing what an hour sitting in here will do.'

Carly shook her head slowly, as though emerging from a dream. 'It's wonderful! The house is so austere-looking outside—and then there's this.'

'Yes, well, first impressions can often be deceptive, wouldn't you agree?' he said gravely.

'I——' Abruptly, she gestured to a bamboo curtain at the far end. 'What's through there?'

Taking her arm, he led her through the room and pulled aside the hanging to reveal a swimming pool, its silky surface reflecting the turquoise and jade tiles that surrounded it. More palms and potted plants were grouped around, and at the side, in front of a pine sauna cabin, were more padded loungers.

'I suppose you swim here every day?' she queried.

'Whenever I can. I like to do fifteen or twenty lengths first thing every morning.'

'Mmm, I envy you,' Carly said, a shade wistfully. 'That's one of the things I miss—I mean, now that they've closed the pool in town for roof repairs,' she added hastily. Somehow, once again, she felt inhibited from saying what she'd intended—that it was the pool back at her parents' lovely Cotswold manor house that she really missed.

'You're welcome to this pool, or the sauna, any time you like,' said Nick.

'Oh, no—no, thank you,' she replied, trying—unsuccessfully, she was sure—to keep the note of horror out of her voice. Swim here? Use the sauna? Share them with him? No!

'Please yourself,' he replied indifferently. 'Now, coffee.'

She followed him back through to the conservatory, where he poured two cups and handed one to her. She lay back on one of the loungers and while he engrossed himself in the contents of a file open on his lap she gazed out idly through the foliage-fringed glass. The view from this part of the house stretched right across the narrow rib of Pennine valley, with Milton in the dip below, so that she almost felt she could touch the opposite side.

'Oh, look!' she exclaimed. 'I can see my house. Over there,' as he glanced up. 'Follow the road out of town, then up past that farm. My cottage is just below that belt of conifers and the open moor.'

'Isn't it a bit lonely for you?' Nick was frowning.

'Oh, no,' she protested vehemently. 'It's marvellous. I turn off the road, down a cart track, and—silence and solitude. It's bliss after 5S have had one of their days, I can tell you.'

She turned to him, pulling a wry face, to find him watching her. Once again there was an intangible something in his gaze that made her skin prickle with tingling excitement, so that all her instincts urged her to leap to her feet and back away from him, her hands held out protectively in front of her.

All he said, rather abstractedly, though, and still without taking his eyes off her, was, 'You're handy for the college, anyway. Within walking distance, I should think.'

'You know it—the college, I mean?'

'Yes. I go there to evening classes.'

'Ah,' Carly nodded. Busy though he was, he must be trying belatedly to make up for having ducked out of school as early as possible. Maybe—she thought of the books in the sitting-room—he was taking a course in English Literature. In which case, whatever her antagonism towards him otherwise, she had to admire him.

'Right. Time to go.'

He drained his cup and stood up, closing the file with a snap. She knocked back the last of her coffee, then went to gather up the two cups.

'Leave them,' said Nick.

'Oh, but surely you expect me to do the washing-up?'

She'd tried to speak lightly, but those disturbing feelings she'd been experiencing every time he came near her gave an acerbic edge to her voice. But he only said impatiently, 'We haven't time. I'll see to them when I get back.'

On the way into town, he was humming as he drove, oozing self-satisfaction, no doubt, at his little victory. It was only as they reached the centre that Carly found herself picking up the tune: 'Me and my Shadow.'

She stiffened; he was obviously trying to needle her again. So the temporary truce, with his gracious offers of taking her potholing or making free use of his pool, was over. Having won their first battle of wills with such little effort, he clearly thought that he had broken her in and she would dutifully toe the Bradley line—like all his women—with no further trouble. Perhaps, even worse, he'd picked up those fleeting moments when she'd found herself succumbing to his undoubted male magnetism, and this of course would only have served to feed his already no doubt highly inflated ego.

Resolutely folding her lips over any remark, she stared straight ahead through the windscreen as he pulled into the car park at the rear of the town hall. He led the way down a corridor, opened a heavy swing door and ushered her into a room where a group of men were sitting around an oval table. Finding herself, without warning, the centre of twenty-odd pairs of appraising male eyes almost froze Carly to the spot and she had to allow Nick to nudge her forward slightly.

There was a chorus of, 'Afternoon, Bradley,' then he said, in a thoroughly formal way, for which she was grateful, 'This is Miss Caroline Sheppard, from the college. She's shadowing me for the next five months, so, with the chairman's permission,' he glanced briefly in the direction of an elderly, grey-haired man, 'she'll sit in on the meeting this afternoon.'

Another chorus of, 'Afternoon, Miss Sheppard', very polite, though Carly was almost positive that she saw two of the men exchange knowing winks and heard, in an undertone, 'When young Nick's finished with her, perhaps he'll send her along to me for a spot of *shadowing.*'

They really were all the same, weren't they—one-track minds? Carly, two angry spots of colour rising to her cheeks, flicked back her hair, muttered a cool, verging-on-frosty, 'Good afternoon,' and dropped into the chair that Nick pulled out for her.

He slid into the seat beside her, so close that his sleeve brushed against hers, but while all eyes were still on them both, quite clearly straining to pick up the slightest undercurrent between them, she willed herself to remain quite still until, as the meeting got under way, she gradually ceased to be the centre of attention and was

able, softly, softly, to inch her chair away from his and
begin to observe the proceedings.

She now realised, that she was not, after all, the only
female present. A middle-aged woman sat beside the
chairman, pencil and notebook poised. Carly smiled
wryly to herself. She had never considered herself a
militant feminist, but really—herself, graciously permitted to 'sit in' on the meeting, and a secretary, de-
votedly taking down every pearl of wisdom that the men
around her uttered. Milton Chamber of Commerce was
obviously fighting a successful rearguard action for male
supremacy.

As the meeting went along—extended shopping hours,
a lengthy but inconclusive report from a group who had
been on a town-twinning trip to somewhere in Sweden,
animated debate over whether the Christmas lights
should be erected in both Clarence Street *and* the Market
Square this year—it soon became apparent to Carly, with
all her senses thoroughly heightened, that Nick was
rapidly becoming bored and irritable.

Heavy sighs, running his fingers through his dark
curls, fidgeting with his pencil until the point broke...
She could only hope that his exasperation was not so
apparent to the chairman, whose eye she caught at that
moment across the table. She hastily gave him a dazzling
smile, as though to compensate for Nick's restlessness.

She was beginning to wonder just why he'd been so
keen to get to the meeting at all, when they at last reached
the final item: a proposed International Trade Fair in
Milton the following summer, and immediately, two
things became apparent to her. First, that Nick was the
driving force behind the whole idea, and second, that
the majority of the members were opposed to it.

Imperceptibly, although he was the youngest man
present, he took the reins of control in his hands. With

supreme self-confidence, he demolished arguments logically and concisely, poured scorn on fears of a financial loss, and generally coaxed and chivvied everyone else the way he intended them to go. Like sheep into a pen, Carly thought. An object lesson in skilful man-management.

At one point, Nick leaned past her, forcibly arguing a point with the hapless man on her other side, and she saw his saturnine face alight with the joy of battle. He caught her eye and gave her a quick, conspiratorial wink.

Smoothing back his unruly curls, he impatiently tugged down his tie, undid his top shirt button, then, struggling in the confined space, began to haul himself out of his jacket.

'Here, let me.'

Without thought, Carly reached across to straighten out the twisted sleeve, but just as she took hold of it he loosed himself with a jerk and his hand came free, his fingers brushing against her arm and sending tingles of electricity right the way up it. Just for a moment, they stared into each other's eyes before he turned away and became very busy peeling out his other arm. Carly, first scarlet, then very pale, shrank back into her chair, becoming aware as she did so of a red-faced man who had just lit up a cigar and was watching her closely, an unpleasant smirk hovering round his fleshy lips.

The door opened and a young girl appeared, wheeling a tea-trolley—subservient female number three, Carly thought ironically—and the chairman, with evident relief, suggested they take a short break. As they got to their feet, though, Nick immediately buttonholed one of the last remaining doubters, and Carly found herself standing next to the red-faced man.

'You feeling all right, lass?' he asked, all solicitude. 'You're looking a bit pale. Nick's a hard taskmaster, you know. Don't let him go wearing you to a *shadow*.'

His tone made Carly's flesh crawl, but she managed a wan smile, only for another man to chip in, 'Yes, I hope he's not putting you under too much *pressure*, Miss Sheppard.'

The chuckles that greeted this sally left her in no doubt as to its true significance. Feeling her colour rising again, she put down her cup and muttered brusquely, 'I'm sorry, but it's rather smoky in here.' And without a glance in Nick's direction, she left the room.

An hour later she was still pacing up and down the car park, when he at last appeared.

'You're still here, then?'

'Of course.' In fact, she had engaged in a bitter internal struggle as to whether to wait for him or not, and had finally decided that it would give him even more satisfaction to find she'd gone.

He unlocked her door and she climbed in. As he started the engine, he remarked, 'Sorry if the atmosphere was a bit much for you in there. Tobacco smoke can be unpleasant.'

'You know very well it wasn't that,' she retorted. 'I just wasn't going to stay there any longer on the receiving end of their—their smutty schoolboy humour.'

'Really?' he said coolly. 'You must excuse our blunt Yorkshire wit—sorry if it isn't subtle enough for your refined sensibilities.'

'It's not that at all. But that—that fat man with the cigar—he's nothing but a dirty-minded pig.'

'George Crosby, you mean.' Nick's laugh grated on her. 'Well, I know he fancies himself as God's gift to women——'

'And you don't, I suppose.'

'—but he's quite harmless,' he continued, ignoring her jibe.

'Maybe. But that doesn't alter the fact that all of them there—they're all chauvinists. They obviously think that this shadowing is just an excuse for toting me round.'

'An excuse for what?'

'For toting me round, showing me off as your—your latest mistress.'

'Oh, for heaven's sake!' The laughter exploded from him this time, but then he glanced at her sharply. 'You really think that, don't you?'

'It was obvious, as soon as I walked into the room.'

'To you, perhaps. But anyway,' his voice all at once softened to a purr, 'is the idea of being my—latest mistress that appalling?'

'I won't even bother to answer that,' she snapped, furious as much with herself now as with him.

She'd badly mishandled the situation—as usual. She knew that. All she'd needed to do, back there in the room, was smile sweetly and make some disarming riposte, subtle enough to take the wind out of their over-weight sails without offending them, but instead of that she'd let the situation get blown up out of all pro-portion—and laid herself wide open to yet more flak from Nick.

Her resentment still simmering, she remarked acidly, as he jockeyed for position in the early evening traffic, 'I suppose you got your own way about the Fair?'

'Of course.' The laconic words said, quite plainly, I always do.

'Don't you ever worry—about putting people's backs up?' She felt real curiosity towards this alien species.

'No.' He sounded genuinely surprised. 'Not when I know I'm right.'

Surely though, somewhere, some place, there just had to be the one person who could put this man down a notch or two—or preferably three or four. Carly just hoped that happy event would occur on a Monday or Tuesday, during the next four months, so that she could be there to enjoy the spectacle. For now, she gave up and switched all her attention to the lighted shop windows and pedestrians hurrying home.

The foundry was in darkness and hers was the only car in the car park. Nick pulled in beside it and after getting out she paused for him to say goodnight. But instead he hurried off up the stairs to his office, so she trudged wearily after him and leaned in the doorway, watching as he flicked through the pile of typewritten sheets which the secretary had presumably left for his inspection.

Finally, with a grunt of satisfaction, he slid them into his briefcase, then as he put his hand on the light switch he seemed to become aware of her.

'What's the matter with you now?' he wanted to know. 'You look as though you've just eaten half a dozen lemons.'

'Oh, nothing. I was just thinking, you didn't really have to drag me up here again. I suppose that's how you intend to do it, isn't it?'

'Do what?' Pattering off down the stairs ahead of her, he sounded thoroughly uninterested.

'Get your own way with me. I mean,' she caught herself up furiously as he turned at the bottom, his brows raised in amusement, 'get me to do as you want—wear me out—exhaust me.'

'*Are* you exhausted? Good heavens.' He looked at her, shaking his head in mock solicitude. 'I hate to worry you, but this has been one of my quieter days.'

Oh, God, Carly groaned inwardly, then stalked off ahead of him as he locked the door. But his much longer legs told and they reached their cars together.

'Fancy a drink?' he called to her, across the roof of his vehicle.

'No, thanks.'

She had to get away from this human dynamo—now, before he wore her down into the dust. She got in and jammed the key into the ignition.

'Start. Please start,' she prayed aloud at the dashboard.

The Mini was well overdue for a service and had been playing up, but this evening it was willing to oblige. Carly reversed out of her space at twice her usual speed, then roared the length of the car park. In her mirror, she could see Nick's lights reflected; they disappeared as he pulled over, obviously trying to beat her to the gate.

She put her foot down to the floorboards and the car leapt through the entrance, nearly brushing the polished red snout of the Aston Martin. Almost shouting aloud with jubilation, she clutched the wheel and raced up the road as though Old Nick himself were after her—well, his near-relative was, she thought with a hysterical little giggle.

But then, as the tidal wave of exhaustion hit her, she sagged in her seat, all her elation gone. Bath, a quick supper in front of the TV and then bed—that was all she was fit for. But then, as she slowed for a halt sign, for the first time in hours the appalling realisation hit her. She'd be back there again, wouldn't she, at seven forty-five tomorrow morning?

CHAPTER FOUR

'COME ON, you evil brute, you, start!'

Carly turned the ignition yet again, but the engine stayed stubbornly silent, not even bothering to cough this time. It was her own fault, of course—she still hadn't got round to that service, and her luck had at last run out. But what a time to choose: ten o'clock on a dark November night. And now that she glanced up, surely those were splodges of rain starting to patter against the Mini's windscreen.

She sat, gnawing on her lip, then got out, slammed the door hard, more to relieve her frustration than to close it, and stood looking around her hopefully in the darkness. But the college car park was almost deserted; she'd stayed too long chatting to Elaine, her class teacher. Ah, well, it was going to be a long walk up that narrow, solitary lane to the cottage. She'd assured Nick Bradley, that first day at his house, that she didn't at all mind the loneliness, but tonight, suddenly, it seemed less than appealing...

Perhaps it was worth going back inside to see if the janitor was still around and could give her a lift. Or maybe—her spirits lightened a little—one of the students from the car maintenance class just might still be there and eager to get in some practical experience.

A gust of wind sent a flurry of dead leaves swirling across the car park and Carly, still sweating from her exercise session, shivered slightly. Hugging her arms across her thin jade velour tracksuit, she hurried towards the main entrance, then stopped, her heart lifting with relief. A man in a bulky car coat had just come through the swing doors at the top of the steps, and she opened her mouth to call to him.

But then, as he came down the steps two at a time, she closed it with a choked little groan and tried to flatten herself into instant invisibility against the skeletal buddleia bushes. But it was too late.

'Carly? Is that you?' Nick stopped on the bottom step, peering through the darkness.

Resisting the urge to say no, it wasn't, she came forward reluctantly into the light.

'What on earth are you doing here?' He surveyed her bedraggled form, smiling faintly. 'Isn't nine til four long enough for you?'

'I've been to my Tai Chi class,' she told him.

'Tai what?'

'Tai Chi. Chinese soft exercises,' she added ungraciously as he stared at her.

'What on earth are those, for God's sake?'

'Movements to harmonise the mind and body,' she said shortly. 'They make you calm and relaxed.'

'Hmm.' He was still studying her closely. 'Been doing them for long, have you?'

'No. I've just started this term,' she began, then realising that, yet again, he was getting at her, she broke off, her lips tightening.

'But I haven't seen you here before,' he queried.

'No, well, it's usually on a Wednesday, but we had to change—just for this week. Anyway, what brings you here on a wet Thursday night?'

'Same as you—I told you I come to evening classes.'

Casually, he held up a book he was carrying and in the light that was filtering down from the doorway she could just make out the title. Her jaw sagged.

'Advanced *Japanese*!' she gasped. 'Whatever are you doing that for?'

'Japan is where some of our market is now, and I intend there to be a great deal more in the future.'

'But you don't have to speak the language, surely? Most Japanese speak English, or else you can use an interpreter.'

He shrugged. 'I prefer to know precisely what's being said when any deal's hammered out.'

What a perfectionist he was, forceful and determined in every aspect of his life. Carly stared at him, that flicker of unease running through her, as it so often seemed to when he was around. What if this laser beam of ruthless determination was ever seriously turned in her direction? Those defences that she'd built around herself—would they stand the onslaught, or would they totter, then crumble into dust? She shivered, and this time not from cold.

'Anyway,' he went on, 'you're going the wrong way. The classes are over.'

'I know.' She managed a cool smile, and planted her feet firmly on the wet gravel. Nothing, but nothing would induce her to ask for his help. She'd walk all the way home on her hands rather. Only a couple of mornings before, when, arms folded and lounging against his own Aston Martin, he'd watched her judder her way into the foundry car park, he'd warned her that she'd better get the Mini seen to pretty soon.

But, she thought resentfully, what time had she had— for that, or anything else—these last three weeks? None. Nick Bradley had seen to that. Her Mondays and Tuesdays had been every bit as hectic as she'd feared, and the rest of her time had been spent either teaching or recouping her depleted energy levels ready for the following Monday.

Behind them, the door banged to and another man, in a navy tracksuit and a towel draped round his shoulders, came down the steps whistling: Rex Sandford, Head of PE at the college and full-time staff-room lecher. But, just now, Carly was delighted to see him. She stepped forward, neatly bypassing Nick's solid frame.

'Hello, Rex.'

He stopped dead. 'Why, hello, Carly darlin'. What are you up to, then?'

She felt his arm snake round her shoulders and just for once, in these extreme circumstances, suppressed the urge to wriggle from under it.

'Have you got your car, Rex?' she asked him.

'Sorry, love, Shanks's pony tonight. Why?'

'Mine won't start.' She dropped her voice to a murmur, hoping that Nick, who was scowling darkly at both of them, would not hear.

'No problem.' Rex's voice too had become an intimate whisper. 'I'll walk you back.'

'There's no need. I'll run you home, Carly.'

Glaring across her head at Rex, Nick put his hand firmly on her arm and for a brief moment Carly felt rather like the rope in a tug-of-war, as a trial of strength took place between the two men, but then Rex's arm fell away. He took his defeat fairly gracefully.

'Well, I'll leave you in safe hands, then, sweetie. See you around, Nick.' And with a brief nod at both of them he had gone.

Nick regarded her, stern-faced. 'What the hell do you think you're up to? That one is married with two kids and another on the way.' Carly scuffed at a dead dandelion growing through the gravel. 'Myumi calls him Octopus Man.'

'Myumi?' She raised her eyes questioningly.

'My class teacher. She's had her own problems with his wandering hands. You're asking for trouble if——'

'I know, I know,' she muttered. 'Usually I run a mile—honestly. But tonight——'

'In any case, you *know* all you had to do was ask me, Carly darlin'.'

The mockery in his voice set her teeth on edge. 'Yes, well, maybe I just didn't want to,' she said truculently.

'Oh, dear. Still sulking, are we, over my having to speak to you on Tuesday?'

'Speak to me? Yell at me, you mean, in front of the entire work force. You called me a bloody halfwit!'

'And so you were. How many times do I have to tell you to wear a safety helmet in the foundry? Sneaking back in, when my back was turned!'

'Well, I wanted to see them bring down the furnace again. I was only in there two minutes.'

'Mmm. Anyway, let's have a look at your car.'

Carly stood in silence as he squeezed himself in behind the wheel and turned the ignition. The engine protested feebly once, then lay on its back. Without a word, Nick extricated himself and strode across to where his car was standing. As he opened the door and got in, the interior light came on, illuminating that dark saturnine face for a few seconds, then went off as he closed the door. She heard his ignition fire, then he reversed at speed out of the parking space.

Her lip drooped. He was abandoning her to a dark, wet walk home, after all. Of course he was. And that was exactly the sort of thing she'd expect from him. All the same, though, she felt a desolate tear well up and trickle on to her cheek.

Angrily she shook her head, then dragged out her sports bag from the rear seat. She was still fumbling for the key to lock the car when the Aston Martin slammed to a halt, its bonnet inches from the Mini's. From his boot Nick fetched out a pair of jump leads, and as she watched he raised both car bonnets and fixed the leads to the two batteries.

'Right, in you get.' But she only stood, not moving. 'Are you going to stand here all night?' His voice crackled with impatience.

'N-no.'

She turned away, but next moment he had caught her by the arm. He put his thumb under her chin and, when she tried to avert her face, tilted it inexorably until it was caught in the beam of his headlights. He stared down at her silently for a moment, then, with a funny little shake of his head, lifted his other hand and gently flicked away that treacherous tear.

'Oh, Carly.' His voice was softer than she'd ever heard it. 'You didn't think I was going to leave you, did you?'

She sniffed, then gave him a wobbly smile. 'I wasn't sure.'

'Well, I haven't. So in you get.' And when she had clambered into her driving seat, 'Now, switch on.'

Miraculously, at the first tentative turn, the Mini's engine fired.

'Keep it going.' Nick's head was bent to the open window, his breath warm on her cold cheek. 'I'll disconnect the leads—it should get you home OK. But get it to Collins's Garage first thing tomorrow.'

'Yes, all right. And thanks,' she added belatedly, but he had already gone, slamming down the two bonnet lids and climbing back into his own car.

She let in the clutch and rather gingerly drove through the car park and out of the gates. Nick's headlights stayed in her mirror as she turned left down the main road. His way home was through town—he must be following her part of the way, which perhaps was a relief.

Advanced Japanese...

So this was how he spent his Thursday evenings. Several times she'd found herself wondering what he was up to between Wednesdays and Sundays...

One morning, cramming bread into the toaster, she'd even found herself gazing across the valley at that four-square Victorian ironmaster's residence and smiling to herself at the thought that the present four-square ironmaster might be in the middle of his twenty lengths... She hadn't been back to the house since that first day. In fact, Nick—apart from the occasional lapse into personal abuse, of course—had been amazingly formal and correct.

He had also kept up his impersonation of a human dynamo. Each morning, when she'd arrived, she'd had not the faintest idea of what was waiting for her: panting behind him on a lightning reconnoitre of the shop floor; sitting alongside him in an update session on the Australian bandstand project; or being whisked off to a sales convention on the other side of the Pennines. And yet, astonishingly, she'd *almost* begun to look forward to Mondays. Nothing to do with Nick Bradley, of course. It couldn't possibly be; it was just being at the sharp end of industry for once, in that noisy, dirty, exciting world. Sometimes a whole day had gone by and she'd realised with a shock, as she'd tumbled wearily into bed, that she hadn't given 5S a single thought...

Nick's father had sat in on some of the meetings. James Bradley was an older edition of his son; stockily built, a shock of wiry grey curls, tough yet humorous face... If you've ever wondered what Nick Bradley will look like at sixty, well, here he is, Carly had thought one day, covertly watching father and son amicably arguing over a point of policy. But I haven't wondered, so there, she'd told herself smartly, and returned to her doodling.

Ahead of her through the flickering windscreen wipers was the dark entrance to the lane. With a wave and a reassuring toot-toot on her horn, she pulled over, expecting Nick to go on past, but instead the powerful headlights pursued her into the turning. She suppressed a groan. Oh, God, he was doing his chivalrous-knight-to-the-rescue-of-the-helpless-little-woman act right to the end!

She accelerated faster and faster up the hill, but when she finally braked at her gate the Aston Martin was right behind her. Scooping up her games bag, she got out, but he was already standing beside his car, a blurred outline in the rain which up here on the fringe of the moors was much heavier.

'Thank you, but you needn't have come so far out of your way,' she told him.

He shrugged. 'Just making sure.'

'Yes, well.' She hesitated, but he still did not seem in any hurry to move. The rain was trickling down their faces. 'Would you like to come in for a coffee?' she heard herself say, and found herself leading the way down the narrow path.

In the porch she was fumbling her key out from the pocket of her tracksuit when she heard him curse softly and turned to see him pushing aside a low-hanging branch and rubbing the top of his head ruefully.

'Oh, sorry,' she said, 'that's my old pear tree. Hence the highly original name.' She tapped the board which was hanging precariously from a nail beside the door and which proclaimed in faded white lettering: 'Pear Tree Cottage'. 'I'm so used to it myself, I just duck underneath. It practically covers the whole wall, but it seems a shame to cut it back. It's a really old variety—*Doyenne du Comice*—they're lovely to eat.'

She knew she was babbling but seemed quite unable to stop. Standing in the narrow porchway, with Nick's frame blotting out the whole night and his head bent towards her to avoid the scratchy branches, she felt even more ill at ease, even though she was now on her home ground.

Smothering her irritation with herself, she pushed open the door and flicked on the light. 'Anyway, come on in.'

The door led directly into the small kitchen. She dumped her sports bag on the unit and stood for a moment trying to regain her composure. But it was very difficult. Here in this tiny room with its low, white-washed ceiling and exposed beams, Nick seemed even larger, his head brushing against the bunches of dried lavender and rosemary which hung down—and even more intimidating. No, it was more than that—he seemed out of place, an alien element in this neat, daintily furnished room, like a full-grown tiger in a toyshop.

He was also, she thought resentfully, as he brushed the glittering raindrops from his black curls, then leaned against the pine table, hands in pockets, taking a casual inventory of the kitchen, thoroughly at his ease, which was a great deal more than she was.

His eyes came to rest on her. 'You're wet through. Go and change.'

'No—no.' Hastily she brushed the silver film of rain from the velour. 'I'm all right.' Her voice was maddeningly high and breathless. 'Let me take your coat, though.'

He slipped it off and she shook it out, then hung it alongside her ancient gardening jacket on an old-fashioned coat rack by the door.

'I-I'll make some coffee.' She flitted past him to the safety of her kitchen cupboards and became very busy reaching down the percolator and two mugs with one hand while with the other trying unobtrusively to prevent her tracksuit from riding up to reveal a segment of creamy flesh.

'Good grief! What's all this?'

She swung round to see that Nick had wandered to the other end of the room and was gazing down at the corner unit.

'Oh, that's fudge.' For the first time this evening her voice sounded natural, she thought with relief.

'Fudge?'

She laughed at his astonished expression. 'Yes, but it's not all for me, I promise you.'

Switching the percolator on, she went across to the unit, where dozens of cellophane-wrapped packets were stacked, while in front of them were several trays of different fudges, neatly marked out and ready to be turned out for packing.

'It's the college Christmas Bazaar tomorrow evening and I said I'd make some for the home-made stall.'

'That lot must have kept you busy.'

'Oh, I've spent each evening this week on it. Not that I mind,' she added defensively as he frowned, though why she should be in the least defensive she really didn't know. 'Anyway, this is the last batch. All I've got to do is bag it up, then I thought I'd tuck a little sprig of this plastic holly into the tie of each packet. Do try some. There's coffee and walnut, or chocolate almond—or that one's rum and raisin.'

'Chocolate almond, please.' He took a piece from the tin and bit into it. 'Mmm—I don't usually go for fudge, but this is delicious!' He gave her a slanting smile.

'You've obviously got hidden culinary talents—or maybe it's only in the fudge line? Plus omelettes, of course.'

Feeling herself colour slightly under that glinting scrutiny, Carly turned back to the stove.

'Well, I did a cordon bleu course when I left school,' she told him.

'And then you changed your mind and went into teaching?' He actually sounded as if he was interested.

'Not really. I wanted to teach all along, but my parents were dead against it. They wanted me to follow some genteel sort of occupation and persuaded me to take the course in Switzerland. My mother was hoping,' she smiled wryly over her shoulder at him, 'that I'd settle for running a fancy little tea-room in Chipping Campden or somewhere. They gave in, in the end, though, and here I am.'

'Yes. Here you are.' And once again she felt the unease rising under his level gaze. 'You know,' he went on casually, 'that's the first time since I met you that you've mentioned your parents.'

'Oh.' She shrugged. 'There's not much to tell. They live near Cheltenham.'

'And I suppose you went to Cheltenham Ladies' College.'

He gave her a baiting look, which she refused to respond to. 'Yes, I did, actually,' she said coolly.

'And what does your father do?'

'He owns a property development business in Gloucester, although he spends quite a bit of his time in London. My mother does a lot of charity work.'

She clamped her lips together. No need to tell him anything else; no need to talk of the empty shell of a marriage, of which she had grown up the innocent victim. The bitterness, the recriminations, the frozen silences, which had made the lovely Cotswold house in its peaceful setting a hollow mockery, and from which since her earliest days she, their only child, had sought refuge riding across the hills on her beloved pony.

Her mouth tightened in the old, remembered desolation and, conscious of Nick's keen dark blue gaze fixed on her, she turned gratefully away as the coffee began to perk. She set a tray with sugar and cream and picked it up.

'Would you like to come through? Oh, I've forgotten the biscuits——'

She swung back sharply—and cannoned straight into him, barely a pace behind her. As the tray lurched, Carly gave a gasp, then somehow steadied it, but not before the jug had fallen, spewing its contents all down him.

For a frozen moment she stared, her hazel eyes widening with horror as the thin cream dripped down what looked like a highly expensive lemon cashmere sweater, to plop from there on to a pair of equally expensive-looking pale grey cords.

The ability to speak finally came back to her. 'Oh no! I'm so sorry,' she wailed. 'Oh, lord, what an awful mess!'

The simmering nervousness she had felt ever since they had arrived at the cottage erupted suddenly into violent action. She banged down the tray, slopping coffee everywhere, and stood for a moment all but wringing her hands. Then, seizing a couple of clean tea-towels that lay on the worktop, she began dabbing frantically at his sweater with both hands.

'I'm so sorry,' she babbled on. 'How stupid of me— I've ruined it!' Lower—lower—then down on her knees she dropped, to mop up the trail of cream which was spreading down his trousers.

And then, quite suddenly, the consciousness of just what she was doing hit her. She was dabbing—no, scrabbling, she realised with dismay, at the area around

Nick's zip and, with just the thin cord between her fingers and his flesh, she was all at once terribly aware of that hard, muscular body, of the lean strength of his inner thighs.

With a faint gasp she sat back on her heels, the scarlet flaring wildly into her cheeks, and looked up, to see Nick, who had not said one word—apart from a muffled exclamation as the cream first found its target—from start to finish, looking down at her as she grovelled at his feet. There was a very ambivalent expression on his face, and suddenly she felt the tension leaping and flickering all around them.

'I think that's about it, thank you.' His voice was cool enough, but there was a barely perceptible tremor in it, which unnerved her even more.

'Er—yes.'

Reluctantly, she got to her feet. On her way up, without thinking, she went to give his stomach area one final scrub, but then all too aware now of the Nick under Nick's cashmere, she withdrew her hand as sharply as though he had unexpectedly bitten it.

'I'm s-sorry.' But she did not look at him.

'So you keep saying.' There was the faintest irony in his voice. 'You know, you really do seem to be making a habit of this. A peculiar phenomenon—every time I come within range, you knock something flying!'

She, though, was quite unable to match his bantering tone. 'Please let me have the dry-cleaning bill,' she said woodenly.

'Oh, for God's sake, Carly!' he exclaimed almost angrily, and snatching the cloths out of her hands he dumped them on the worktop. 'There's still enough coffee left, so just get some more cream, will you?'

'Yes—yes, I will,' she mumbled. 'You go on through to the sitting-room and I'll follow you in.'

When he had gone she leaned against the table, trying to steady her breathing, which had become erratic and flurried. Her hands too were trembling, sending little tremors up her arms. She forced herself to take several long, slow breaths, counting up to ten with each, then refilled the jug, tipped out some oatmeal crunch biscuits on to a plate and carried the tray through.

Nick was standing with his back to her, looking at the small oak cabinet where she kept some of her treasured possessions.

'I gather you like paperweights,' he remarked with a grin.

'However did you guess?' She pulled a face, and the tension between them seemed to recede a little. 'Yes, I've loved them ever since I was a child.'

She set down the tray and, going across to him, opened the glass door.

'That's the first one I ever had. It's Victorian, I think.' She picked up the small glass dome and handed it to him. 'My grandmother gave it to me when I was about ten. That's a picture of Weymouth on the bottom—she'd taken me there for a holiday that summer. You can see the pier, and the donkeys on the sand—look.'

She bent over it just as he leaned forward, so that her hair, falling over her face, brushed against his and she drew back abruptly.

'And this one,' hastily, she reached another, much larger one, from the shelf, 'I had for my twenty-first birthday.'

'Mmm, it's beautiful. But it's modern, surely?'

'Yes. It's Caithness glass.' Carly cradled it in her hands. 'I love it. I always imagine it as being the centre of an ice-cap. See—it almost smokes with cold.'

Slowly she traced the swirl of deep purple amethyst which enclosed a central core of icy white fire suspended in the glass, then glanced up at him.

'Yes, it's wonderful.' But his eyes were fixed not on the paperweight but on her face, and she set it down with a little clatter.

'Oh, and here's another one—you'll be interested in this.' She was babbling again; she knew she was.

'Good heavens!' Nick peered down at the small globe she was holding out to him. 'It's the Brontë sisters, isn't it?'

'Yes. It's from the portrait done by their brother. A friend of mine got it for me from Haworth when I was still at college.' Being so near to Nick, virtually trapped between him, the sofa and the cabinet, was doing funny things to her pulse rate again. 'Let's sit down, shall we?' she went on in that infuriatingly breathy voice. 'The coffee must be getting cold.'

She indicated the two matching chintz-covered arm-chairs, and as Nick sat down, stretching his long legs comfortably out in front of him, she perched in the other chair facing him.

'A biscuit?' she asked.

'Please. Home-made cordon bleu, I suppose?'

'Well, home-made—but hardly cordon bleu, I'm afraid. I don't really bother all that much, just cooking for myself most of the time. Cordon bleu beans on toast or spaghetti bolognese is about all I usually bother with. Still, at least my training's coming in handy tomorrow evening.'

'The fudge, you mean?'

'Well, not really.' Carly smiled spontaneously, actually beginning to relax a little. 'There's going to be an auction at the bazaar and six of us staff are going to be sold off to the highest bidders. You know, offering our skills,' she went on hastily, as Nick raised a quizzical eyebrow. 'Rex Sandford is donating eight hours of free football coaching. Diane Wellings—she teaches art—is going to do a portrait of whoever bids for her—and I'm offering to cook a cordon bleu meal.'

'That sounds fun,' he remarked drily.

She grimaced. 'Well, I'm not really looking forward to it—the auction bit, I mean. But it's all in a good cause. It's in aid of a new college minibus—the other one collapsed in a heap months ago. And if we get one, I'll be able to take 5S out at weekends.'

'Weekends? That's a bit over and above the call of duty, isn't it?'

'Certainly not. I don't mind how much time I give up for them,' she retorted, fighting down that defensive tone again.

'And what will you cook?' Nick set down his mug and leaned back in his chair, watching her.

'Oh, they choose. Although knowing 5S, it'll probably be along the beefburgers and hot dogs line!'

'5S?'

'Well, yes.' She grinned. 'Unofficially—and strictly off the record—I gather that half a dozen of them are pooling their finances to get me. I hope they manage it—I'll enjoy giving them a treat.'

'Hmm.' He regarded her unsmilingly. 'You know, you are one hell of a lot too close to those kids of yours.'

'And what's that supposed to mean?' Carly responded instantly to the censorious note in his voice.

'Precisely what I said. You're too close, too involved. They're very nearly your whole life.'

'And why shouldn't they be?' The unwise words had tumbled out before she could prevent them.

'Do you really need me to spell it out for you?' Nick looked at her, his eyes narrowing. 'Good God, I do believe you do.' He sighed faintly. 'You shouldn't get too involved, my dear Carly, because children grow up and grow away. It's part of life—of living. Parents have to learn that hard lesson, and so do teachers—if they've got any sense in their beautiful, stubborn heads, that is. Any other way lies heartache.'

There was *something* in his tone—sadness, maybe? Certainly he sounded as though he pitied her, for heaven's sake. 'Oh, if that's what's worrying you, please don't,' she snapped. 'I'm quite aware that 5S will be leaving school in July. But I shall pick up the third year in September, and go through with them for three years.'

'And then another 5S, and then another. So you're going to settle for a series of sterile relationships all your life.'

'Sterile?' She flushed angrily.

'Well, what else is it? My definition of a sterile relationship is one which can't grow, can't develop. Of course, on the other hand,' he paused, 'you don't take any risks that way. Is that it, Carly, are you taking the easy way out?'

She stood up abruptly. 'I'll run my life the way I choose,' she said tautly. 'And now, if you'll excuse me, I've got to bag up the rest of that fudge.'

But he did not seem to hear her, much less take the unsubtle hint. 'Tell me, why do you think you were put forward for this shadowing scheme?'

She stared down at him, her anger dissolving into puzzlement. 'Well—because of the jobs, I suppose. A lot of my kids will hope to get work in the local foundries and so on, so when I volunteered——'

'Volunteered? That's not exactly the impression I got when you first turned up on my doorstep.'

'No, well,' she floundered, 'Miss Davis, the last principal, she asked me, so——'

'Precisely. And from what I've heard of Jean Davis, she's a remarkably shrewd woman. Hasn't it ever occurred to you that you just might have been selected because she could see what you're incapable of seeing?'

'And what's that?'

'What I said. You're too emotionally involved with them. Good grief, girl, you can't think about anything else!'

'No, that's not true—it really isn't.'

'Isn't it?'

'No——' But she bit her lip on the rest of the sentence. She couldn't possibly tell Nick Bradley, of all people, that just lately—on some Mondays and Tuesdays, at least—5S *had* occasionally slipped away from her mind. He could easily misconstrue her words— and it simply wasn't worth disproving his point at the expense of inflating his already massive male ego.

She glowered down at him in silence for a moment, through the fringe of fair hair that had fallen forward over her eyes, then muttered, 'I really must get on with that fudge.'

But as she went to go past him to reach the door, with a half-smothered oath he sprang to his feet and, seizing her by the wrist, swung her fiercely round to him.

'What the hell do you——?' was as far as she got before his mouth came down on hers. Caught off balance as she had been, in the middle of an angry exclamation, her mouth was open. She tried to close it, to bring her teeth together in self-defence, but too late. Nick's lips, warm and strong, were sealed to hers, his tongue probing the soft moistness of her mouth. She struggled to breathe, but only felt his breath enter her.

The fury was sizzling in her. How *dared* he do this to her? She tried to jerk herself away, but he put his free hand around the back of her head, his fingers tangling brutally in her hair so that tears of pain sprang to her eyes. As she wriggled in his arms, desperate to break his grip, he caught her to him, his fingers splayed across her lower spine, moulding her to him, compelling in her an awareness of every contour of that superb, hard, wholly masculine body. Her breath caught in her throat, in a little sound that was half sob, half helpless rage. Nick's eyes were on her, so near that she could all but feel the angry desire that blazed in them.

Her own lashes fluttered down and she closed her eyes. But immediately she was conscious only of the sweetness of his mouth, the feel of him, the smell of him—warm, male and vibrantly alive—that filled her nostrils, and far, far worse, the strange, intoxicating sensations which he was engendering in her own body by way of response.

But then, even as her knees began to buckle, the anger reasserted itself. With a desperate wrench of her head, she freed her mouth and, bringing up both her hands, pushed him away from her. For one split second there was a silence so profound that she could hear the almost soundless ticking of her gilt carriage clock and then the world was filled with her own ragged, indrawn breath.

'H-how dare you?'

'Very easily.'

He seemed perfectly unruffled, which inflamed her anger still further. And yet—was he? There was a dusky flush along his hard-edged cheekbones, a tautness around his mouth, that suggested—Carly closed her mind to what it suggested, and, summoning all her depleted resources, thrust her chin proudly in the air.

'I think you'd better go, don't you?' She used the special voice which she kept in the freezer compartment of her fridge, specifically for dealing with men like this, and he responded instantly.

'What's the matter, Carly? Scared that one honest-to-goodness kiss might knock your careful equilibrium out of the window?' His eyes roamed around the room, deliberately taking in the paperweights, the rows of pretty china on the shelves, the porcelain bowl of rose-scented pot-pourri, the antique framed sampler on the wall, then his lip curled with cool contempt. 'All right, I'll leave you in your solitary, *sterile* ivory tower, then.'

In the kitchen, he snatched down his car coat, but then paused in the open doorway. 'Oh, and Teach——' she winced at his tone '—don't forget to pull up the drawbridge when I've gone. The real world's out there, you know, and I'd hate to let it in.'

She stood, leaning against the table and staring unseeing at the opposite wall until, even when she strained her ears, the sound of his car had faded away to nothing. Then slowly she straightened up. Her face was bruised, her lips still burning from his kiss. Savagely, she dragged the back of her hand across her mouth to wipe all memory of it away. But even as she did so, she smelled the smell of him, faint yet indelible, still lingering on her cold skin.

CHAPTER FIVE

'AND now, ladies and gentlemen, lot number six. Last but not least, we come to this delectable little filly.'

The auctioneer took a firm grip on her wrist and Carly, a self-conscious smile tacked precariously to her hot face, allowed herself to be paraded to the front of the stage, to a chorus of wolf whistles and loud foot-stampings—no doubt from 5S.

'What could be nicer, ladies and gents? Just take a look at those well-turned fetlocks!'

Carly gave him a look which she had at least *intended* to be amiable, then, as he released his grip, retreated to the side of the stage, where she stood, half hidden by the blue curtains, nervously running her hands down the unpressed pleats of her coral-pink wool dress. It had been considered a stroke of incredible good fortune that Joe Blaydon, the auctioneer at Milton Cattle Market, should be a leading light of the College's Parent-Teacher Association, but all the same...filly...fetlocks——

'But tonight you aren't bidding for her good looks——' a chorus of groans to which Carly responded with a sick smile '—but for her superb culinary skills. For the lucky highest bidder, Miss Caroline Sheppard will cook a splendid cordon bleu meal. Through your generous support, we've already raised seventy pounds, so let's see if we can make it three figures. Now, who'll start us off?'

'Five pounds!' The shout came from the side of the hall, and Carly suppressed a smile as she recognised the voice of Barry Jones, ringleader of the 5S group.

'Six.' A voice she didn't recognise.

'Seven.' Barry again.

'Eight.'

'Nine.'

'Ten.'

A new voice had chipped in, and Carly, all ears, gave a start of alarm. It couldn't be... But when she peered round the curtain into the crowded body of the hall she saw that Rex Sandford, who had already been through his ordeal and been auctioned for twelve pounds, had pushed his way to the front.

There was a slight hesitation, then, 'Eleven,' from Barry.

'Twelve.'

Oh, please, Carly was praying silently, her hands tightly clasped in her pockets, please let the boys have scraped up enough money. *Don't* let him win—or if he does, let his wife and two children, and another on the way, not be away for the weekend... Glancing down, she caught a glimpse of Diane Wellings, also now safely in the front row, and the art teacher rolled her eyes at her commiseratingly.

'Thirteen pounds.'

Yet another voice had cut in, and against the little murmur of interest that rippled round the hall, Carly recognised the clipped tones of the principal, Dr Jutson. She really did not know whether to be relieved or appalled. What was it to be—the frying pan or the fire?

'Fifteen.'

This from Rex, and Barry, after a hurried consultation with his cohorts, dropped out with a shrug of resignation, leaving the two men to raise the bids rapidly to twenty-nine pounds. And what was even worse, although on the surface the bidding was thoroughly good-humoured, it surely must have been obvious to everyone in the hall that the struggle was developing into a deadly serious battle of wills, and Carly, set-faced, could only stare at nothing, all her attention strained to the next bid.

'Do I hear thirty pounds? Just one more pound to make the grand total three figures.' Joe Blaydon, lynx-eyed, stared round the crowd, then focused on Rex. 'It's with you, sir—the gentleman with the orange tie.'

Rex, who had been looking increasingly sour, hesitated, but then opened his mouth.

'Thi——' he began, but he never finished the word.

'Five hundred.'

From the rear of the hall the voice cracked out like a whiplash. There was a moment of utter, stunned silence, Rex's jaw dropped into a foolish gape, then there was an audible gasp of astonishment and heads swivelled.

Carly herself, probably the only one in the hall to recognise the voice immediately, broke out in a cold sweat and shrank back with a half suppressed groan of anguish. She didn't believe it—she couldn't believe it! She shut her eyes, shook her head hard to try to clear it, then opened her eyes again.

The auctioneer had finally recovered his voice. 'Five hundred—did you say five hundred, sir?'

'Yes.'

'Pounds?'

'Of course—unless you prefer guineas?'

'No—no, that's fine.' And without even a glance at the two erstwhile rival bidders, he banged down his gavel before shouting above the babel of talk and laughter that had broken out, 'If the gentleman would please come to the front of the hall. Oh, Mr Bradley. Sorry—I didn't recognise you.'

And as Carly watched, breath suspended, the crowds parted to allow Nick, immaculate in fine-knit navy polo sweater and tight grey trousers, to saunter through.

She ran the tip of her tongue round the outline of her dry lips, and felt once more, as she had done a hundred times since last night, the slight puffiness where his mouth had bruised the delicate flesh. She was almost sure, although it was quite impossible—she'd scrubbed her face a dozen times since—that she could taste him on her skin. Maybe he *was* indelible—maybe that was how he marked his women—maybe she had an invisible Nick Bradley brand on her, and now he'd come to claim his property.

As a hysterical laugh welled up inside her, she turned to fight her way through the swirling folds of curtain, only to bump straight into Diane.

'Oh, Carly—poor you!' The other girl pulled a comical face. 'But still—*five hundred pounds* for the minibus fund! That's great, and—well——'

'Well what?' Carly demanded, not quite liking her knowing wink.

'Well, I mean—wow, he is two hundred per cent real man, is Nick Bradley. He is one gorgeous hunk——'

'Did I hear someone mention my name?'

From just behind her, right on cue, came a smooth-as-silk voice, but she steeled herself not to turn. Diane, though, was quite unabashed. Flinging back her auburn curls, she shot Nick a wicked glance.

'I was just saying, lucky old Carly. I'm only sorry you weren't bidding for me. Still, any time you want your portrait painted, just say the word—and it won't cost you five hundred pounds either.'

'Thank you, Diane. I'll bear that in mind.' He nodded in graceful acknowledgment, but mercifully did not allow his eyes to slide in Carly's direction. She'd always envied

her friend's talent for chatting up men, sparring, flirting
with open enjoyment, but just now she wished that Diane
were marginally more discreet.

'But now, if you'll excuse us both——' and, taking
Carly firmly by the arm, Nick led her back to the waiting
Joe Blaydon, and she was forced to stand, a sickly smile
on her scarlet face, enduring even more of the auctioneer's idea of humour, while Nick counted out wads of
money. He hadn't even got the grace to pay discreetly
by cheque or credit card! she thought, as the impotent
fury simmered inside her. Like a customer in some
Eastern bazaar, he was rapidly slapping down one
twenty-pound note after another, as if to show the whole
world that he was buying her—and for cash down.

Finally he walked her down the steps into the hall, his
hand on her arm again in what must have looked like a
thoroughly proprietorial manner. His fingers were
digging into the soft flesh and, glancing down, she saw
the tiny bruises already springing up.

'Let me go, will you?' she hissed through her teeth,
before throwing a dazzling smile in the direction of a
group of openly staring sixth-formers.

'Certainly not. I want to talk to you.'

Steering her towards the relative seclusion of the rear
of Father Christmas's Grotto, Nick pushed open an
emergency exit and thrust her ahead of him out into the
deserted car park. After the warmth of the hall, it was
chilly here in her thin wool dress, and she hugged her
arms across her chest as she swung round to face him.

'You're mad—you know that? Totally, utterly mad!'

'Oh, I don't think so.'

He was enjoying this—every pore in his body was
exuding hateful, smug, *masculine* self-satisfaction. But
why had he done it? Was it—was it some kind of twisted,
public revenge for her response to his kiss? Or—she

swallowed, having been thwarted in his desires last night—and she could no longer hide from herself the awareness that he *did* desire her sexually—was he now using this devious ploy to get his own way with her? Somehow she had to stand firm against the overpowering tide of his personality.

'You realise,' she snapped, 'you've made me the laughing-stock of the whole of Milton?'

'You know, Carly,' a more serious note momentarily entered his voice, 'you really must stop fretting about what other people think of you.'

'But five hundred pounds!' she wailed in an anguished undertone.

He shrugged. 'Well, Joe was asking for three figures.'

'But you didn't have to bid that much. You were just showing off.'

He looked pained. 'I never show off. And anyway, maybe I think you'll be worth every penny.' He slanted her another of those ambivalent smiles, but she pretended not to see it. 'Besides, it seemed the quickest way of bringing the whole unedifying spectacle to an end—those two scrapping like a pair of stray dogs over a particularly juicy bone. You might at least be grateful to me.'

'*Grateful!* For what?'

'For saving you from a fate worse than death. Which would you have preferred—fifteen rounds with Octopus Man or a fight to the finish with Doctor Deep Freeze?'

There was a glint of humour in his dark sapphire eyes again. He was inviting her to laugh with him, she knew that—but she was quite unable to. She was probably mishandling things yet again, she thought sadly. If only she could be like Diane and treat the whole thing as the marvellous joke that most people clearly saw it as, but she was now so ill at ease with him—every nerve-ending in her so aware of the slightest movement of that powerful body, so conscious of every nuance of expression, that she could scarcely meet his eye, much less unbend enough to share this particular joke.

'If you'll excuse me,' she said stonily, 'I'm going home now. I'm very tired.'

'Can I give you a lift?'

'No, thank you, I've got my car. And yes, it did go into the garage today.'

'Good,' he said smoothly, 'but you're not going quite yet. I've bought you, remember.'

'Not for tonight, you haven't.'

'No,' he acknowledged, but before she could even begin to warm at her little triumph, 'For tomorrow, though.'

A strangled sound came from Carly's throat, which just might have been, 'Tomorrow!'

'Of course.'

'But that's impossible! I——'

'You remember that first day, when you promised to do me a five-course meal some other time?'

'I did no such——'

'Well, tomorrow's that other time. And just in case you're worried about your reputation——'

'What reputation?' She gave a mirthless laugh. 'I've already lost that tonight, thanks to you!'

'——you'll be very well chaperoned by Messrs Sawamura, Kikukazu and Machido.'

Carly, her jaw sagging, stared at him as a feeling of unreality crept through her. 'What on earth are you talking about? Who are they?'

'Three of Japan's top businessmen. They're over here on a buying trip and I aim to spend this weekend convincing them that a range of cast-iron Victorian-style conservatories like mine is just what they need to take their company to the top of their country's interior design tree. My housekeeper has been getting in such a flap at the prospect of catering for them that I've packed her off for the weekend, so——'

'So you want me to cook for them?' she said slowly.

'It seems the ideal solution. English-style will be fine— or French,' he added briskly. 'I don't suppose your course ran to Japanese cooking.'

'Not really,' she said non-committally. 'And suppose I don't agree?'

'Ah, well.' He sighed regretfully. 'I'll just have to go back to Joe and tell him the deal's off. I suppose he could always auction you all over again.'

'You know I won't go through that again, damn you!' Impotent fury raged in her, as she was torn between the desire to leap at him and pummel that navy sweater as hard as she could and sit down on the ground and burst into loud, uncontrollable sobs. 'And anyway, I can't deprive them of the chance of the minibus.'

'That's right. I knew you'd be sensible.'

A horrible thought struck her. 'Did you know about this auction before——' her eyes slid past his '—last night?'

'No.'

So, single-handed—or rather, single-mouthed—she'd landed herself in this. 'And just what were you intending to do with them before this bright idea struck you?'

'I was taking them to dinner at the Country Club. But this is a much better arrangement all round, don't you agree?'

Carly did not reply—and yet surely, if she allowed herself to think coolly, he was right. He was offering her a straightforward business deal, from which both sides would benefit. And really, it was quite flattering that he should entrust her with such a vital role in what was clearly an important occasion for Bradley and Son.

She sighed inwardly. If only he weren't so high-handed, constantly rubbing her up the wrong way. It was stupid really: he made her so grouchy all the time, like a snarling little wildcat who bit his hand any time it came within mauling distance of her mouth... No one had ever had this effect on her before—she was normally quite sweet-tempered... It was him—his fault entirely. And yet could it be that her reaction to him was a disguise for the terror that one day, when her guard was down, he might be the first man to breach her defensive wall?

Her fingers clenched into tight balls so that the nails bit into the skin, but then, all at once conscious of Nick's piercing gaze, she struggled to at least half pull herself together.

'Your businessmen—what time are they arriving?' she asked.

'Not till the afternoon, but I'll pick you up at eight-thirty to take you shopping. I hope that's convenient,' he added casually.

'Well, actually I was planning on a lie-in after tonight, and then I was going to start decorating the spare bedroom.'

'Ah, well,' he dismissed the spare room with a wave, 'you can do that next week. Oh, and by the way, bring an overnight bag with you.'

The alarm bells jangled again. 'But I'm only cooking Saturday dinner,' she protested. 'I'll wash up and then you can run me home.'

'Uh-uh. I'm not risking breaking the mood when they've been softened up by your no doubt superb meal by leaving them alone to take you home. That's when I aim to move in for the kill. No, it's much better if you stay.'

In the half darkness she saw him glance quickly at her, then quirk an eyebrow. 'Oh, Carly, surely you didn't think I was intending to get you under my roof and then do a Rex on you?'

'N-no, of course not.' Relief was flooding through her and yet, in a strange way, mingled with the relief was a feeling almost of let-down.

'You needn't have worried, my sweetie. I'm not in the habit of taking women by force, and I don't intend to make a start with you. I'm far more inclined most of the time, anyway, to put you over my knee and spank you, but when I do make love to you——'

Carly, who had just fished out her car keys, dropped them. Nick stooped and retrieved them but then enclosed the keys and her cold hands in his warm ones, so that she could not draw back.

'When I do make love to you, Carly——' this time, his voice sank to a soft caress that wound itself round her like silk '—I promise you it will be with your willing co-operation.'

She wanted to say, Good, because in that case, it will never happen in a month of Sundays. But under the spell of his voice and his touch, the words just would not come out.

'Eight-thirty sharp, then.'

He released her hands, and as they fell to her sides he turned and strode away in the direction of his car.

It was, in fact, eight twenty-nine by her kitchen clock when the rat-a-tat sounded. Carly was just folding her PVC apron and went to the door with it still in her hands.

'You're up, then.' Nick, sleek in a cream Aran sweater and dark grey tweed trousers, raised one black eyebrow by way of greeting.

'You sound disappointed,' she retorted. 'I suppose you were hoping you'd have to drag me out of bed.'

'Drag you out? Oh, I don't think I'd want to waste my energy like that, Carly.'

He grinned at her and, to her chagrin, she felt the colour immediately rising in her cheeks. She had in fact been wide awake since five, and among the conclusions she'd come to as she'd lain waiting for the dawn was that if she was going to get through this appalling weekend unscathed she was not—repeat *not*—going to allow herself to be got at by *him*. And now, with her very first words, she'd thrown herself wide open to attack.

Picking up her lengthy shopping lists, she jammed them into her shoulder-bag.

'I hope you've got plenty of money with you, plus your credit cards,' she said stiffly.

'Of course. Why? Do you want me to buy you some sexy silk undies?'

Oh, God, she was going to have to guard her tongue every time she opened her mouth today. He was in an utterly impossible mood—and she knew why, of course. He'd won her, bought her, got her over a barrel, and there was absolutely nothing she could do about it— except be perfectly cool and unruffled by whatever little witticisms he chose to come up with.

'I'll just get my coat and case,' she said, curling her lips into a saccharine smile, then gestured to the containers which were lined up on the table. 'Could you take these out to the car, please?'

'What—all of them?' Nick surveyed the bulging cardboard boxes, plastic carriers and wicker picnic hamper with astonishment. 'I have got the odd saucepan, you know.'

'Yes, but a good cook always prefers her—or his, of course,' that cool smile again, 'own utensils. Oh, and be careful with that one, please—there are some break-ables in it.'

'Yes, ma'am.' And, scooping up several of the boxes, he returned to his car.

That's the way to do it, Carly my girl, she thought. Brisk and efficient—that was all that was needed to keep him well and truly in his place. As she combed her silky, new-washed hair, and smoothed down her workmanlike black and white check wool shirt-dress, she permitted her reflection in the bedroom mirror a little smile of triumph before she slipped on her pale blue mohair jacket, picked up her case and went back down to the kitchen.

As they drove down the narrow lane, she asked, 'What time are you expecting them?'

'Oh, not till about three. I thought we could give them tea, coffee or whatever they want when they arrive—served in the conservatory, of course——' he slanted her a grin '—then I'll take them down to the foundry, show them some of our other products, and I've set up a meeting there with Giles and Ray. We should be back for dinner at about seven-thirty. OK?'

'Yes, that's fine.' Inwardly, Carly breathed a sigh of relief. She'd been going to insist on having the kitchen to herself while she prepared the meal, but this way there was no chance of Nick keeping a close, unsettling eye on proceedings under the guise of helping her out. 'And when are they leaving?'

'Their hire car is coming for them at ten-thirty on Sunday morning—they're going on up to Scotland from here, I gather.'

'Oh, so you'll be able to get me back home by lunchtime.'

He shook his head. 'No. I've moved that Country Club booking to Sunday lunch—for the two of us. After they've gone, I'll either want to celebrate or cry in my soup—and, either way, I'll prefer company. That suit you?'

'I suppose so.' It hadn't of course occurred to him that she might be much happier, having fulfilled to the letter the terms of their agreement, to spend what remained of the weekend catching up on her own affairs. As she digested this latest example of his high-handedness, a thought that had been niggling at her mind ever since his plan had been sprung on her surfaced once more.

'These businessmen—they'll probably wonder who I am, and—you know, what our—relationship is.'

Nick swung out into the main road, then threw her a swift glance. 'Well, I was thinking of introducing you as my own personal geisha girl.'

'You—you wouldn't!' She gazed at him, aghast.

'Why not? It's no more than they'd expect, I'm sure.'

'Well, in that case,' she spluttered with outrage, 'you can just turn the car round and——'

As, far from braking, he accelerated, she banged her hand down on the steering wheel, but he brushed it aside.

'Oh, Carly, why is it that with you, more than any other woman I've ever met——' he paused and she sat, terror-struck by the thought of what he might be about to say '—I have this uncontrollable urge to light the blue touch paper and then retire—pronto—out of range?'

As she stayed mute, he added casually, his eyes fixed firmly on the road ahead. 'The only thing is, I have the strangest feeling that one day, unless I'm very careful,

I may not retire quickly enough to avoid considerable damage to myself.'

Just for a moment his eyes slid to meet hers, and she saw in them an expression which she had never glimpsed before, and which set her pulses unaccountably jangling. For the remainder of the journey she engrossed herself in her various shopping lists until Nick parked just off the bustling square.

'Right. Where first?'

She pursed her lips. 'The supermarket, I think.'

He locked the car, then, his arm resting on her back, steered her across the busy road towards the store. It was surprisingly pleasant to have that masterful arm round her, guiding her through the stream of traffic, her cheek brushing against his shoulder in its chunky sweater. Stop it! she told herself sternly. Cool and businesslike, remember?

But then it felt equally pleasant, a few minutes later, to be wheeling the laden trolley together, just like the dozens of other couples also engaged on their weekend shopping. Oh, yes, she reminded herself scornfully, as she took a packet of farmhouse butter from the cold cabinet, and then they'll be going back to the behind-the-scenes rows, the searing quarrels without which no marriage is complete, is it?

She jerked the trolley into the queue at the butchery counter.

'I suppose you weren't thinking of doing roast beef, were you?' Nick asked hopefully.

'Possibly,' she replied evasively. 'Why?'

'Well—roast beef and Yorkshire pudding. There's nothing quite like it.'

'For a Yorkshireman, anyway,' she laughed. 'So the old saying's right, in your case, then.' As he raised his brows questioningly, 'You know—the way to a man's heart is—I mean—— '

Her voice trailed off abruptly as she realised what she was about to say, and she became very busy studying the rows of joints, barely speaking another word until they had loaded the food into the car boot.

'What now?' asked Nick.

'Round to the market.'

In the entrance to the covered market she paused and pulled out a list. 'Would you get these fruit and vegetables at that stall, please?'

He glanced down the list, then pulled a face. 'But I can't possibly get all this on my own!'

'Yes, you can,' she said firmly.

'Where are you off to, then?'

'Oh, here and there.' She gestured vaguely.

'In that case—— ' Nick pulled out his wallet and thrust several notes at her.

'Thanks. I shan't be long.' And she plunged off into the crowds.

In the far corner of the market there was an excellent new wholefood and delicatessen store that she'd earmarked as her prime objective, and when she finally emerged loaded with carriers he was already back at the car. She gave him the receipt and, in spite of his protests, carefully counted out the change.

'Right. That's it,' she said, and went to get in.

But he put his hand on her arm. 'Just one more thing.'

This time he led her along the pavement, down a recently renovated mews just off the square, and stopped outside a small, discreet shop. In the window was one beautiful silk blouse, the price tag turned inwards, and a tasteful arrangement of lace-frothed bra and suspender belt. Oh no! He hadn't been *serious* about those silk undies, had he? Carly clutched protectively at her neckline.

'What have you come here for?' she demanded, a tremor in her voice. 'It's—it's a dress shop.'

In fact, it was currently *the* dress shop, to where the most expensively dressed women from all over Yorkshire were finding their way.

'I know. I'm buying you a dress to wear tonight.'

A dress? Well, that was something, at least. But even so——

'No, you're not!' Her voice was sharp with alarm. 'I've got a perfectly good one in my case. It's a new one, so don't worry, I shan't let you down.'

'I'm quite sure you wouldn't,' Nick said smoothly, 'but for tonight I want you to wear something of mine. After all, for this weekend, remember, you belong to me.'

Inside her neat black patent shoes, she felt her toe-nails curl with terror. 'No, I don't want you to. *Please!*' She ran her tongue round her lips, ash-dry with panic.

'Yes.' Quite immovable, he inclined his head.

He tightened his grip on her elbow and as Carly seemed to have lost the use of both her legs he was able to lead her over the step. Despair was sapping at her, but still she had to fight him.

'Huh! Any time, I suppose, you'll be telling me that this weekend I'm Bradley's——'

'Woman. Exactly.' It was a velvety purr. 'I couldn't have put it better myself.'

PLAY
HARLEQUIN'S

LUCKY HEARTS
GAME

AND YOU GET

★ **FREE BOOKS**

★ **A FREE GIFT**

★ **AND MUCH MORE**

**TURN THE PAGE AND
DEAL YOURSELF IN**

PLAY "LUCKY HEARTS" AND YOU GET...

★ Exciting Harlequin Presents® novels — FREE

★ Plus a Crystal Pendant Necklace — FREE

THEN CONTINUE YOUR LUCKY STREAK WITH A SWEETHEART OF A DEAL

1. Play Lucky Hearts as instructed on the opposite page.

2. Send back this card and you'll receive brand-new Harlequin Presents® novels. These books have a cover price of $2.99 each, but they are yours to keep absolutely free.

3. There's no catch. You're under no obligation to buy anything. We charge nothing — ZERO — for your first shipment. And you don't have to make any minimum number of purchases — not even one!

4. The fact is thousands of readers enjoy receiving books by mail from the Harlequin Reader Service. They like the convenience of home delivery. . .they like getting the best new novels months before they're available in stores. . .and they love our discount prices!

5. We hope that after receiving your free books you'll want to remain a subscriber. But the choice is yours — to continue or cancel, anytime at all! So why not take us up on our invitation, with no risk of any kind. You'll be glad you did!

THE HARLEQUIN READER SERVICE®: HERE'S HOW IT WORKS

Accepting free books places you under no obligation to buy anything. You may keep the books and gift and return the shipping statement marked "cancel". If you do not cancel, about a month later we'll send you 6 additional novels, and bill you just $2.44 each plus 25¢ delivery and applicable sales tax, if any.* That's the complete price—and compared to cover prices of $2.99 each—quite a bargain! You may cancel at any time, but if you choose to continue, every month we'll send you 6 more books, which you may either purchase at the discount price ... or return at our expense and cancel your subscription.

*Terms and prices subject to change without notice. Sales tax applicable in N.Y.

CHAPTER SIX

'RIGHT, here we are.' Nick shouldered open the door and dumped her case—and that navy and gold carrier, with its tissue-wrapped contents—on the single bed. He nodded towards another door. 'Your bathroom's through there—I hope this is OK for you.'

'Oh, yes—yes, it's fine, thank you.'

The room was attractively furnished in light wood, with soft greens and pinks, and with a dormer window looking out over the garden and beyond to the autumn bracken on the moors, but Carly was now in such a state of nervous tension that she was barely aware of anything.

'We'll probably stay on late downstairs talking business, but with you up here on the top floor, you should be able to get your beauty sleep undisturbed.' He gave her one of his sideways smiles. 'I'll finish unloading the car, then—get everything into the kitchen for you. Although if I'd known how much you were bringing, I'd have hired a fork-lift truck!'

As soon as he had gone, Carly kicked off her high-heeled shoes and went through to the bathroom, where she splashed her face with cold water in an effort to clear her mind of the confusing emotions that were swirling around in it. Another of her five o'clock resolutions had been that, having been landed with this ordeal, she'd show Nick Bradley that she was worth every last penny of the ridiculous sum he'd paid for her. She would be the absolute height of efficiency, bringing every strand of her highly expensive culinary course into play to turn herself into a Supercook for this weekend, at least, and she was going to need the clearest of heads to achieve all that.

Back in the bedroom, she slipped on a pair of old espadrilles, then scraped back her hair into a rubber band and twisted it into a knot tight enough to match the severe lines of her dress. Just for a moment she paused by the window, looking out abstractedly, then squared her shoulders and went back downstairs.

Nick was just carrying in the last of the boxes when she reached the kitchen.

'Shall I help you unpack?' he asked.

'No, thank you.' Not looking at him, she reached for her apron, put it on and tied it very firmly. 'You can leave me now—I can manage. Oh, just one thing. I couldn't get any rice wine this morning.'

'*Sake*, you mean?'

'Yes—so could you look out a very dry white wine, please?'

He pursed his lips. 'A Chablis, do you think?'

'Yes—that'll be fine.' Carly turned away and began busily unpacking the nearest box of groceries.

'Well, I'll leave you to it, then. Shout if you want me. I'll be in my office at the end of the corridor.'

'Mmm.' She barely answered him.

Instead of going, though, he came up behind her, and as Carly went rigid she felt his finger twine itself gently into one lock of hair that must have escaped her band.

'Relax, sweetie,' he murmured. 'Everything'll be fine, I'm sure.'

Relax? With Nick's hip brushing softly against her, his breath warm against her neck?

'I'm *p-perfectly* relaxed,' and she jerked herself away.

'OK, OK.' He held up his hands in a placatory gesture. 'You're perfectly relaxed.'

As soon as the door closed behind him, Carly swiftly completed the unpacking, finally removing from the bottom of one of her boxes a large book. She laid it on the table and patted its cover. This was it—her secret weapon—*The Complete Illustrated Oriental Cookbook*. She had bought it in a book sale the previous summer but had never even opened it until last night, when she'd spent several agitated hours poring over its contents before at last deciding on two main courses: a delicious-sounding Beef *Teriyaki*, and *Goma Yaki*—chicken breasts with sesame seeds. That would provide a choice, in case the guests had different preferences—although she could guess which Nick would go for, even if there wasn't any Yorkshire pudding to have with it.

She was taking a terrific risk, she knew. She'd never made either of these dishes before, or anything like them, and on any normal occasion she'd have given herself at least one practice run, preferably two, but this was anything but a normal occasion. Suppose the meal was a total disaster? Suppose the three men flounced off, leaving Nick minus a half-million-pound order... There'd be only one person to blame, for him to vent his anger and frustration on... The razor-sharp knife with which she was cutting thin slices from the two-pound piece of best fillet beef slipped, taking a transparent sliver of skin from her first finger.

It wasn't too late. She'd got all the ingredients to provide something as secure and tested as a chicken or beef casserole... *No*. She'd made up her mind that she was going to show Nick Bradley, and that was precisely what she was going to do.

At one o'clock, she put a bowl of vegetable soup, two fat rounds of toasted cheese sandwiches and a glass of cold milk on a tray and went in search of Nick's office. When she went in, he was seated at a desk awash with a sea of files and papers. He had thrown off his sweater and rolled his shirt sleeves up, and every glossy black curl stood on end, where he had been rumpling his fingers through them.

Carly stood behind his chair, staring down unseen at those endearing curls—and particularly that small one that curved into his nape—and as she did so, strange, unrecognisable sensations stirred into life inside her. Next moment he must have sensed her presence, for he swung round, giving her a tetchy scowl, and she set down the tray and fled.

Two hours later, she stood back, wiping the back of her hand across her hot face and surveying her preparations. The first course, a delicate beansprout soup, was ready. Ideally, it should have been cooked last thing, but her confidence was shaky enough already, without that. Besides, having given herself two main courses to prepare at the last moment, she couldn't have coped with soup at that stage as well.

For now, though, she thought, gnawing her lower lip anxiously, everything was done that could be done. The sliced beef and chicken, glossy with marinade, lay ready in their dishes; the carefully prepared garnishes of spring onions and celery were keeping fresh in a bowl of iced water; while the two lovely old Worcester china *compote* dishes which she'd tracked down in one of the cupboards were piled with the fruits that would form the dessert—black hothouse grapes, mangoes, mandarins and crisp Cox's orange pippins—and stood by the open window for coolness.

She opened the door of the stove and took out the last tray of scones, pale gold, and set them on a cooling rack, then turned to the table where she had laid out the rest of the tea-things: dainty cucumber sandwiches, a rich moist fruit cake and a featherlight Victoria sponge, hidden under tea-towels in case Nick should come bursting in... *Tea, coffee or whatever they want when they arrive*... She smiled to herself in almost childish glee at the thought of the full-scale English country house tea she'd be presenting as Phase One of her 'Showing Him' campaign.

Her ears caught a faint crunch of tyres, then she heard Nick bounding downstairs. Zero hour. Swallowing down the butterflies, she smoothed back another stray strand of hair which had escaped, exchanged the espadrilles for her high heels, and opened the kitchen door.

Nick, who had changed into a formal dark grey suit, was ushering into the hall three smartly dressed men, each clutching an executive case. As Carly approached, rather diffidently, he turned.

'Ah, good. Gentlemen, may I introduce Miss Caroline Sheppard. *Kochira wa Sheppard Caroline san desu.*'

As they each bowed low and took her hand, she smiled and said, *'Hajime machite.'*

From under her lashes, she sneaked a quick glance at Nick and saw, with a little spurt of smugness, that his jaw had dropped. He wasn't the only one—though she had now exhausted the sum total of *her* Advanced Japanese, the fruits of a quick scamper through to the sitting-room and a furtive riffle through his Japanese textbook.

'I do hope you had a good journey,' she went on. 'Perhaps you'd like to go through to the conservatory and I'll bring tea.'

When she wheeled in the loaded trolley, she gave Nick another sidelong glance. After one startled look at its contents, he shot her a secret 'well done' smile, which warmed her. He seemed quite at ease already, sitting back in his padded chair, making small talk, and yet, knowing him now as she did, her antennae could pick up the small, tight coil of tension deep inside him. This weekend obviously mattered a great deal to him. Was it the money—this order opening the gates to many others, perhaps? Well, yes, but much more, it was, she was sure, that driving determination not to be thwarted in any goal he set himself.

Whatever the reason, her need to make a success of this weekend for the sake of her own pride all at once, incredibly, seemed to become intertwined with an equally fierce desire to do whatever she could to help him. Perhaps, together, they really could charm these particular birds out of the trees.

She leaned forward, smiling warmly. 'More tea, Mr Kikukazu? And do have another scone—or perhaps a slice of sponge?'

She heard the car door click and, peering out of her bedroom window, saw Nick escorting the three men in through the front door. A few moments later came the sound of voices from the floor below; they must be coming up to change for dinner.

Carly glanced at her watch. Just after seven. She'd give herself another five minutes, then go back to the kitchen for the final bout of high-speed cooking. This was when disaster really could strike...

To subdue the panicky fluttering under her midriff, she walked across to the full-length mirror. But that was a mistake, for it brought her face to face with her other self, a self dressed in a slink of a strapless black velvet dress which outlined each curve of her body so that it became a seduction of flesh. Oh, from a distance—as she gave it a fleeting, nervous glance—it looked fine, with its modest, up-to-the-neckline-and-down-to-the-wrist inset of black lace, but through the lace could be glimpsed an alarming amount of pale cleavage, while she knew that if she turned sideways—she didn't turn, but it was there all the same—she would see the wicked plunge from nape to waist.

In the shop that morning, as Nick had looked on with obvious impatience, she had gathered together three of the most harmless-looking dinner dresses and was already homing in on a pretty polyester two-piece when he had removed it from her hands and tossed it back on the rail.

'Try that one,' he'd commented, and she'd turned to see—this dress. She'd deliberately tried on the other three first, then finally, reluctantly, slipped it on...She'd almost been afraid to venture out of the changing-room.

'Yes, that's the one,' Nick had said, after a long look which made her body all but break out into a rash of prickly heat.

He was already halfway to the cash desk when she'd put her hand on his arm. 'I prefer that blue dress. This one—well, it's——'

'Provocative? Yes, isn't it?' he'd drawled, his cat's smile rasping on her jag-edged nerves.

'It's worse than that!' she'd hissed, all too conscious of the discreetly veiled glances of the assistants. 'It's—it's downright blatant! I never wear clothes like this.'

'Well, maybe you should. Anyway, you can stop arguing—this is what you're wearing tonight.'

And Carly, as one more straw of feeble resistance was torn from her grasp, had given way into silent, seething acquiescence.

Now, as she forced herself to confront that stranger in the mirror, she felt her heart beat a little faster and her pulses flutter. Had Nick been right, after all? The black velvet set off the creaminess of her skin tones, she couldn't deny it, while her hazel eyes glowed with subdued fire, and her fair hair, newly washed and caught up into a simple chignon, framed perfectly the long elegant neck, the delicate bone structure of her face.

But even so... I like to look ladylike, she thought despairingly, and I don't tonight. You certainly do not, a small voice said in her ear.

Abruptly she turned away, then caught sight of the glass standing on the dressing-table. Earlier, she had found a bottle of cooking sherry in one of the kitchen cupboards and on an impulse—certain that she was going to need a shot of Dutch courage—she'd sneaked a glassful up with her. Now she drank it with a grimace of distaste, then, as it hit her stomach, she drew a deep breath and, carrying her black evening shoes, padded softly downstairs.

She had almost reached the hall when above her she heard a footstep and swung round to see Nick, coming down at his usual two-at-a-time pace. He did not see her at first, but when he did he halted for a moment, looking down at her, then came on more slowly and stood a couple of steps above her, regarding her. He had changed into a dark blue velvet evening jacket, with a frilly white shirt and bow tie, but the soft evening light filtering through that wonderful stained window above their heads, which was lighting up her face, left his in deep shadow so that she could not see his expression.

But there was something—a sensation—emanating from him that turned her throat dry. She shouldn't have had that sherry—it was doing peculiar things to her, making her breathless, dizzy, so that she wanted all at once to lean towards Nick, put out her hand and——

The hand, already moving, jerked back to her side and she cleared her throat, a hoarse sound. 'You—you look very nice,' she said in a feeble imitation of her own voice.

'Thank you. So do you. I was quite right, you see.' But he did not return her tremulous smile.

'H-how did it go at the foundry?' she asked.

'OK, I think. Ray and Giles did a great job.' But he sounded preoccupied. 'Carly.' He stepped down and put his hand on her arm so that little pinpricks ran up and down it.

'Yes, Nick?' she whispered. He was going to——

A door opened on the first-floor landing, and his hand slid away.

'I was coming down to see if you need any help.' His voice was brisk now, but still did not sound wholly under control.

'Oh—no, thanks. Don't worry.' She managed a taut smile. 'Everything's fine. If you like, you could light the candles on the table—I've put some matches in there. I did all the rest while you were out.'

'What would I do without you?'

The jades and ambers of the stained glass played on his face, turning his eyes silvery-violet so that once again it was impossible to make out the expression in them.

'Oh,' she said, her voice uncertain again, 'you'd have managed, I'm sure.' A light footfall sounded on the stairs above them. 'Well, I'd better get back to the kitchen.'

'Yes, all right. Oh, and Carly——' as she turned back to him, he gave her a swift, conspiratorial wink '—good luck!'

Carly took a pear from the dish and sat back, peeling it. All her fears had been unfounded; whether it was a well-timed burst of adrenalin, or the combined effects of cooking sherry and Chablis, she didn't know—and didn't care—but she was floating through the evening, and actually, amazingly, enjoying it.

Of course, she told herself cynically, there was no reason why it shouldn't have gone well. After all, she'd grown up seeing dinner parties like this practically every week, with new—or potential—clients to be wined and dined and coaxed by her father; while her mother, a coolly elegant older version of herself, played her role superbly, sitting across the polished rosewood table from her husband, yet divided by far more than a beautiful Coalport dinner service, gleaming silver, and the perfect bowls of hothouse flowers which she had personally arranged...

Carly realised with a start that Mr Machido was speaking to her and she came gratefully back to the present. The conversation had flowed easily—all three men spoke excellent English—but by seemingly tacit consent there had been no business talk tonight. To her relief, Nick had obviously explained her situation and they were eager to learn her reaction to the shadowing.

'Oh, it's been most——' she darted a quick glance at Nick, one of the rare times she'd actually met his eye during the meal '—illuminating.'

They also, apparently, all had school-age children, and questioned her at great length on the merits of the English educational system, but now, over the dessert, she had allowed herself to slip slightly into the background as Nick regaled them with an enthusiastic account of the joys of potholing.

Suppressing a shudder, she leaned forward to take a small bunch of the black grapes. At the same instant Nick, still talking animatedly, reached out for an apple. Their fingers touched, their eyes met in startled awareness, then both sharply withdrew their hands, he to continue smoothly with his description of his most recent dive, she, very pale, to sit back, her breathing fast and shallow, her heart thumping under her ribs so loudly that it seemed impossible that no one else could hear it.

As her fingers toyed with the smoky-black grapes, she realised with horror that her gaze was being drawn inexorably back to Nick. How good-looking he was... In the glow of candlelight, with the velvet jacket and snowy frills of shirt front, he looked—a faint smile lifted her tight mouth—every inch the successful Victorian ironmaster.

How strong, how *alive* he was! And yet that same aliveness had an animal quality, a virility that suddenly terrified her. She stared at him in fascination, unable now to tear her eyes from him, and felt, for the first time in her life, the throb of intense sexual awareness of another human being take hold of her body.

Her hands shook and, wrenching her gaze from him at last, she saw that she had crushed the grapes she was holding to a pulp. Hastily she dropped her hands to wipe them on her napkin under cover of the table, as fear flickered through her—fear of herself, fear far more of Nick. If he should discover how she felt—but he mustn't. She had to make very sure that, in spite of his razor-edged perceptiveness, he never guessed at her feelings.

'I'll help you with the coffee, Carly.'

Her busy fingers, pleating and unpleating her napkin, froze for an instant.

'Oh, no—no. I can manage.' She smiled brilliantly. 'If you'd all like to go into the conservatory, I'll bring it through.'

But as she finished stacking the plates in the dishwasher, she heard Nick come into the kitchen. After one swift glance, she kept her attention firmly on setting out the coffee things on the tray, only asking, as casually as she could, 'How do you think it's going?'

'I'll tell you tomorrow.'

But she could sense the bubbling elation behind the laconic words and could almost feel it as he came and stood beside her. Somehow, though, she managed to go on automatically setting out the cups and saucers, and he continued. 'But off the record, it's going marvellously—thanks to you. You know, if we do pull this off, you deserve fifty per cent of the profits.'

'Oh, you've paid more than generously for my services already.' She wanted to sound tart, but could not wholly suppress the glow of pleasure at his words. In any case, he ignored her response.

'You know, Carly——' he flicked a spoon against the sugar bowl '—we make a great team, you and I. Can't I tempt you?'

'T-tempt me?' She took a step away from him.

'Yes. Out of teaching.' A swift look from those sapphire eyes. 'What did you think I meant? You're wasted on 5S—a beautiful, poised hostess,' he did not seem to notice her wince, 'a superb cook. That cordon bleu course of yours must have been first-class—and it really did include Japanese cookery.'

'Well, actually,' she could not resist a little smile, 'it didn't. This is the first Japanese meal I've ever cooked.'

'Good heavens!' Nick looked at her with open admiration. 'There you are—you see what I mean? They've taken it as a tremendous compliment that you've laid on this meal for them. In fact, one way and another, everything's looking just great.'

'I'm so glad, Nick.' And she was, genuinely. She turned to him, her eyes shining, but then, at the expression in his eyes, she felt her stomach muscles contract. 'The—the coffee's ready.'

But as she reached for the percolator, Nick's hand arrested hers. Once more she seemed to lose all powers of resistance as he turned her to him and with his thumb began to trace along the outline of her dress, where the black velvet met the lace on the curve of her breasts.

Her head bent, she stood helplessly watching that thumb unhurriedly brushing across the lace, first over one breast and then, as the rise and fall of her breathing grew quicker and quicker, the other. Finally his fingers rested in the shadowed valley between them, so that she could feel their touch warming her skin, sending ripples of sensation prickling along every blood vessel, every muscle, until her whole body was heavy and torporous.

Surely he must be able to feel the pounding of her heart—and surely it was *his* heart that she could feel, beating through the pulse in his thumb which still lay across her breast? She felt as though she had been too long under water, with all the oxygen driven from her body. She had to break free from him, or she would drown! Taking in a long shuddering gulp of air, she stepped back, to fetch up hard against the stove.

'Sh-shouldn't you be getting back to your guests— you know, moving in for the kill?'

Nick's own breathing was ragged, but then, as it at last steadied, the faintest hint of a smile quirked his lips. 'Yes, you're quite right—as ever, Carly. In for the kill.'

He picked up the loaded tray and, with hands that were still not quite under control, she took the coffee-pot and followed him out to the conservatory, grateful for its cloying warmth to excuse the hectic flush on her cheeks.

CHAPTER SEVEN

'GOODBYE.' Carly gave a last wave as the hire car swept off down the drive, then next moment it had rounded the rhododendrons and was gone.

'Phew—thank God that's over!' Pulling a wry face, Nick let out the heartfelt exclamation. '*Not* the most relaxed weekend of my life.'

'But is it all right? About the contract, I mean.'

Carly's voice was tight. This morning, she'd seen very little of the way things were progressing, for after preparing a light breakfast she'd left them to it. Now, she turned to him anxiously. She had lain awake for hours, long after hearing them come upstairs, fretting about the outcome—although, in the dark early hours, she had had to admit to herself that a lucrative business deal was way down in the reasons for her wakefulness. But even so, it would be such an anticlimax if it had all slipped through his fingers at the last minute.

By way of reply, Nick pulled a folded sheet of paper from the inside pocket of his jacket and, as he brandished it triumphantly at her, his face broke into an irrepressible grin.

'You mean, they've already signed——' she began, her eyes sparkling.

'Signed and sealed, my sweetie.' And before she could even tense, he had snatched her up in his arms, crushing her to him in an exuberant hug, and kissed her full and long—and very hard—on the mouth.

When they finally broke apart, Carly clung to him helplessly, her eyes blank, and for a moment his grip tightened again before he released her abruptly. Running his fingers through his black curls, he turned towards the house.

'Hell, I feel like a steel spring that's just been let loose! I guess I was even more wound up about this weekend than I thought.' He shot back his cuff. 'Half-past ten—plenty of time before we go to the club. What do you want to do?'

What she desperately wanted to do was run upstairs, collect her case, which had been packed since seven o'clock that morning, and have him drive her home. She could no longer seek refuge behind her poised hostess mask—not now, with the guests gone and Nick and herself alone in this huge house...

'L-look, Nick.' She moistened her lips. 'I'm sure you're busy, and I've got loads I ought to be doing at home. So, if you'd rather——'

'Nonsense. Of course you're not going home.' He caught sight of her face and frowned impatiently. 'And what's wrong with that?'

'Oh, nothing. Just, why do you always have to be so—so bloody *imperious?*'

'Imperious? Me?' He looked genuinely astonished. 'And anyway, even if I am, maybe it's the only way I can get anywhere with you. But no arguing,' as she opened her mouth, 'after everything you've done this weekend, it's the least I can do. But it's still too early to get ready. I tell you what—let's have a swim.'

'A swim? Oh, no—I mean, I'm sorry,' she even managed to infuse genuine-sounding regret into her voice, 'but I haven't got my swimsuit with me.'

'So? Need that matter?' His eyes were daring a response from her. 'Well, you can always wear your bra and pants.' But then, before she could react to that, 'I know—Simone left her swimsuit last time they were up here.' His eyes skimmed down her figure and up again. 'Yes, you're about her size—I'll fetch that for you.'

And ten minutes later, Carly was once again peering anxiously into her bedroom mirror. Nick had called the absent Simone's costume a swimsuit, which to Carly's mind meant a one-piece, unremarkable and definitely non-eyecatching. In fact, what she was now wearing were two slivers of wet-look gold satin which did not so much hide as reveal the crucial areas.

Never had her legs appeared as endless as they did in the cutaway style of the pants, never had the full curve of her breasts been so provocative, and never, without her actually being naked, had so much creamy flesh been on parade. It was positively indecent. What was he trying to do to her? First that dress and now this——

Well, she wouldn't wear it. Swallowing down the hard knot of pure terror which was rising from her stomach to her gullet, Carly put her hands resolutely to the thong ties at the sides of the pants. But then they paused. Nick had decreed that she should swim, so swim she would, willing or no—and clothed or no—and in that case the sooner she got it over with the better. Brazen it out— and if she hurried she could be safely in the water before he appeared.

Avoiding her reflection, she dragged back her hair, catching it up into a ponytail with a rubber band, then, putting on the pretty white broderie anglaise housecoat she had brought with her, she snatched up a large bath towel and ran helter-skelter down the stairs and through into the conservatory.

Parting the bamboo curtain with one tentative finger, she peeped through. Good, she'd beaten him to it. She pushed through, but then, as the beads jangled softly, Nick's voice came from almost at her feet.

'About time.' He had been treading water in the deep end out of her line of vision, but now he swam away from the side. 'Thought you'd changed your mind.'

'Of course not,' she said coolly.

'Well, come on in, then.'

'In a minute.'

She stood fingering the pink ribbon ties at her neckline, then walked halfway down the pool, conscious at every step of his eyes following her. She dropped her towel on one of the recliners, turned her back to him and, with shaky hands, began to undo the little pearl buttons of her housecoat.

Behind her came a splash, and peeping under one arm she saw that Nick was doing a rapid crawl away from her. She tore the ribbons apart, pulled off her housecoat and, crossing the tiled floor in two quick steps, flung herself straight into the turquoise depths.

When she surfaced, she saw that Nick was still carving his way through the water with powerful strokes, seemingly oblivious to her presence. As his fingertips touched the rail, he jack-knifed round in one fluid movement and headed back down the pool. Getting in his twenty lengths, she thought with a wry smile, as, with much more sedate strokes, she swam towards the far end.

'Fancy a drink?'

She hadn't heard him, but now, as she spun round, she saw that he had cruised in alongside her.

'Coffee?'

'No—not coffee.' He jerked his head, the black curls plastered sleekly down to his skull, and for the first time she saw the silver ice bucket standing on a low table by the side of the pool. Her eyes widened.

'Champagne?' she asked.

'Of course.'

Champagne? On a practically empty stomach—and after the effect that that one glass of cooking sherry had had on her?

'Oh, not just now, thanks. Er—later, perhaps.'

'Please yourself,' Nick said indifferently. He eyed her as she bobbed in the water alongside him. 'You swim well——'

'Thank you.' She didn't know he'd been watching her.

'—for a girl.'

'Well, of all the——' She stopped squeezing water out of her ponytail and glared at him. 'If it comes to that, so do you—for a conceited male chauvinist—— Aah!'

As he made a determined grab at her, she gave a shriek and squirmed out of reach. Flinging herself over on to her stomach, she set off in a frantic crawl, hurling over her shoulder, 'Race you to the deep end!'

She was clutching for the bar with a triumphant, 'I've——' when she felt her ankles snatched in a vice-like grip and she was being towed rapidly backwards.

'You—you cheat!' The exhilarated laughter broke through her helpless spluttering and swinging herself round she lunged at him, pushing his head beneath the surface. 'Race you to the other end!' And she was off again, sheer terror adding wings to her flailing legs.

'Beat you!' She made a victorious snatch for the rail, but then, as she turned round, her shout of triumph faded. Nick was nowhere to be seen; the entire surface of the pool was empty, except for the wake left by her frenetic dash. Oh, God, she'd drowned him——

'Got you!' Nick must have swum the whole length underwater and now he'd surfaced, shark-like, right beside her, grabbing her round the midriff. 'You can't keep a good potholer down.'

'Oh, you!' She laughed with relief. 'You did that on purpose to—to scare me!'

'Now, would I?' Devilment danced in his eyes but then, suddenly, the laughter vanished. 'Carly. Oh, Carly.' His grip tightened and she felt herself being drawn to him.

'No, Nick, I——' But his mouth came down, his lips hard on hers. His arms were holding her against him, their legs were intertwined, wet skin dragged against wet skin as if their flimsy swimsuits no longer existed and their bodies were melting, merging into one——

She jerked her head back. 'No!'

Bringing down her elbows with all the force she could muster, she broke his grasp and sent him momentarily off balance. Before he could recover, she hurled herself up the steps, seized her housecoat and, clutching it to her, ran along the side of the pool and crashed headlong through the bamboo curtain into the conservatory.

Her breathing was harsh in her ears, her arms and legs rasped against the fronds of the tropical plants, but she had her hand on the catch of the glass-panelled sliding door when she felt herself caught up in a pair of strong arms.

'Let me go!'

She clawed despairingly at the door, but Nick lifted her clean off the ground. He swung her right round before setting her on her feet once more, holding her gently but inexorably by the elbows so that she was forced to stand facing him.

'Oh, Carly!'

There was bubbling laughter in his voice and she sensed him regarding her lowered head. She wanted to struggle, but there was no point. For an instant, her glance flicked up, but then, horribly conscious of that almost bare body—clad only in the briefest of black trunks—inches from her own, she had to keep her gaze fixed on the floor. There were her feet, her toes—pale, slender, pink-tipped. But there, one black marble tile-width away, were Nick's bare feet, tanned and strong, and his legs—no doubt, if she dared look, every bit as intimidatingly masculine as the rest of him.

She swallowed, then said gruffly, 'W-what do you want?'

Putting one hand under her chin, he forced her face up, his fingers sinking into the soft skin as she resisted.

'Look at me, Carly. *Yes,*' as she murmured protestingly and finally she had to raise her eyes to meet his. In them, she saw the desire which she so feared—but also a warm tenderness which made her heart contract painfully for an instant.

'My beautiful girl,' Nick said softly, and her eyes widened, then flickered down to be veiled by her lashes. 'What I want is—this.' He reached up and, releasing her wet hair from the band, ran his fingers through it, letting it fall on to her shoulders.

'And this.' Her pulses fluttered as, splaying his hands under her chin again, he brushed his thumbs lightly across her full lips until her mouth went dry, then ran them unhurriedly down the column of her neck to rest against the wildly beating pulse at its base.

'And this.' With endless slowness, he slid one thin gold strap from her shoulder and, as the breath caught in her throat, let his fingers trace its path, his thumb brushing so gently that she could scarcely feel it over the upper curve of her breast.

With one part of her brain, she registered that he had released his hold on her. All she had to do was turn and run. And yet... And yet, as his hands, his voice wove their hypnotic spell, she was powerless to break free and she knew that she must stand there forever, submissive to his will.

'And this.' He lowered his mouth and kissed her, his warm lips sliding enticingly to and fro over hers, inviting her to share his pleasure, and with a little murmur she opened her lips to him and let him gather her unresistingly into his arms. The kiss was long, and when at last they broke apart they stared, almost startled, into one another's eyes.

'Oh, my sweet!' He gave her a rather shaken little smile. 'You know, I think you've far more power over me than is good for you—or me.'

Putting up his hands, he untied the side thong of her bikini top and it fell away to reveal the lovely full curve of her breasts. She heard him draw a shuddering breath, then very slowly he brushed the flat of his hand across first one breast, then, as that tautened into life against his palm, the other.

Very deep within her something ignited, something which was taking her far beyond rational thought, so that she wasn't any longer the cool, controlled Carly Sheppard, but a totally new being—a wanton, seductive woman revelling in the intoxicating power of her body.

'Nick.' It came out as a breathy little sigh and she swayed towards him.

Scooping her up into his arms, he carried her across the tiles to the rear of the conservatory. Shouldering aside some of the lush-growing ferns and sweet-scented shrubs, he knelt down and set her on a pile of hammock cushions.

She lay there, her hair splayed around her as, still kneeling, he gazed down at her. The stern lines of his face were softened, there was a flush on his cheekbones, on his lips a tender half-smile, while his body—for the first time, she allowed her eyes to stray down his strong neck, across the silky brown shoulders, over the powerful breadth of chest. His waistline tapered to a flat stomach and she could see the vertical ridges of muscle running down. So, hidden beneath those suits and chunky winter sweaters, was this—perfection of form. And below that again——

She swallowed and, dragging her eyes away, put up her hand and shyly brushed it across the fine dark hairs on his chest, feeling as she did so the skitter of his heart. He seized her hand and bit gently into the palm.

'Carly,' his voice was muffled so that she could scarcely hear it, 'what a dance you've led me! I've wanted you since that very first day when you flounced into my office doing your prissy little schoolmarm act.'

He smiled at her, a smile of lazy triumph and his hand moved caressingly, possessively across her stomach. *Possessively!* Carly's eyes, half closed under the spell of languorous sensuousness, flickered then flew open.

'No!' Thrusting his hand away, she rolled across the cushions until she was wedged up against the rough trunk of a palm tree. He reached for her, but she pushed him away and scrambled on to her knees.

'Leave me alone, you—you——'

'What the hell's got into you?' Nick, his face still flushed, gave her a thunderous scowl.

'Oh, you nearly managed it, didn't you?' She clawed for her housecoat and held it to her.

'Managed what, for God's sake?'

'To s-seduce me. You've been determined to have me—you've just told me that—and everything you want, you've got to have, no matter what anyone else might w-want.'

'Now look——' His cheekbones were dusky with anger now, but she was past fear.

'You—you're no better than Rex Sandford, do you know that? Oh, you may be able to throw more money around—you may be able to *buy* me—but really you're as big a rat as he is!'

'Why, you——'

'You just wanted *me*. Nothing of what I might want or not want—nothing about l-love——'

'Love!' He almost flung the word back in her face. 'What the hell do you know about love? Very little— apart, that is, from those bloody school kids of yours. They get all the love—and the loving—that a cold-hearted little bitch like you is capable of giving anybody. But they can't hold you in their arms, make that beautiful ice-cold body tremble——'

'Don't be disgusting!'

'Disgusting? Yes, that's what it is to you, isn't it? You feel nothing of the warmth, the pleasure, the joy of giving pleasure.'

'Surely, you mean *taking* pleasure. That's what you intended, wasn't it? That's what this whole weekend's been leading up to—a cosy little seduction scene. Champagne by the pool, that dress, this sexy bikini— and how do I know it's Simone's? You probably keep it handy for any of your little bimbos who may need *warming* up a bit before you start on them!'

She drove through his ferocious retort, the anger— with herself at least as much as him—making her voice savage. 'Well, sorry to disappoint you, but I don't succumb that easily.' And the fact that she *had* almost succumbed put an even sharper edge to her tongue.

Nick got to his feet and, his hands clenched, took a step towards her. For a terrifying second she thought he was going to strike her, but then, his lips tightening into a thin line, he said curtly, 'Go and dress. It's time we were getting ready.'

'I'm not going to the Country Club.'

'Oh, yes, you are.' His voice was grim, and she had to force herself to stand up and face him squarely, for the expression in his eyes made her stomach muscles contract with fear.

'I will not go,' she said clearly and distinctly. 'Please take me home.'

Eye met eye in a battle of wills, then his mouth twisted into a sneer. 'What's the matter?' Every word was a grey pebble dropping into icy water. 'Frightened I might fall on you in the club lounge, tear your clothes off you and rape you on the Axminster?'

'Just take me home, please,' she said coldly. 'Or, if you'd prefer, I'll call a cab.'

Nick muttered something under his breath and gripped her wrist. Carly flinched, fearful of what he might be about to do. After all, she'd thwarted him, and who could tell what his reaction might be? But then he dropped his hand.

'All right.' The contempt in his voice made her cringe inwardly. 'I'll take you back to your ivory tower—where you belong.'

He slid back the glass door, gesturing her through it with an ironic courtesy that grated against her nerve ends and, with a haughty tilt of her head, she walked past him on unsteady legs.

Nick jammed on the brakes, coming to a halt outside her garden gate, and Carly felt weak tears of relief spring to her eyes at the sight of her home. But she blinked them back hard. Soon—very soon—she would be able to let them flow, but not now, not in front of him.

Without breaking the brittle silence which had reigned since he had handed her into the car as formally as though she were a stranger, she put her hand on the door catch.

'Not just yet. Oh, don't worry,' as she tensed, 'I'm not about to leap on you.'

But the anger had gone; there was only a kind of weariness in his tone, and when, startled, she turned in her seat, his eyes were bleak. Something in his expression and the taut lines of his pale face touched her with a kind of guilty anguish that surprised her into speech.

'Nick, I'm——'

'Are you going to spend the whole of your life like this?'

So he was back on that theme, was he? Her lips tightened. 'Why not? It may be very difficult for you to understand, but not every woman is desperately yearning for her life to revolve around Nick Bradley. And so——'

'Be quiet!' He put up his hand and laid it across her mouth, the gentle action shocking her into silence far more effectively than a slap would have done. 'I don't just mean with me.' He gave a faint smile. 'Astonishing as it may be to you, I really do know that I'm an arrogant, high-handed bastard. No, I mean with anyone.'

'And what makes you think that I need anyone else to make my life complete? I'm happy—perfectly happy,' she added, so there could be no possible doubt, 'with my life the way it is.'

'Are you, Carly? Are you quite sure about that?'

'Yes, of course I am,' she retorted belligerently.

'All right. If that's the way you want it.' He got out and opened the boot. 'Go and unlock the door, while I start to bring in your stuff.'

It seemed to take hours to carry in all her cooking gear, which just the previous morning she'd loaded with such bubbling excitement—and by the time every last box was back on her kitchen table, she felt as though her nerves were all but twanging like overstretched violin strings.

'Thank you,' she said stiltedly, still speaking to the spot just behind his left shoulder, as she had been ever since they'd got out of the car.

'Right, then, I'll leave you to it.' He turned towards the door.

But she didn't want him to go like this—not after the laughter, the comradeship, the triumph they'd shared, before it had all been turned to ashes. If only she could have—— *No.* Carly pulled herself up sharply. It wasn't her fault. If only he'd been content to leave everything the way it was...

'Oh, one thing.' Nick paused in the doorway. 'I presume you'll want to give up this shadowing business.'

'Of course not.' She set her chin proudly. 'I'll see you at the foundry as usual tomorrow.'

He regarded her bleakly for a moment, then nodded and went out, closing the door behind him.

Carly slumped down into a chair and leaned her head on her hand. Oh, God, what had she done—or almost done—amid that sensuous, scented warmth? All but allowed herself to be seduced. No, you didn't, she told herself in a searing flash of insight, it wasn't Nick—she'd been horribly unfair to him. It was her. *Something*—something dark, something terrifying had woken deep inside her like a sleeping serpent, stretched and uncoiled itself.

Oh, Nick was dangerous, she knew that. She was frightened of him—of the power he threatened to exert over her, the power to set her calm, well-ordered life on its head. He had almost invaded her—literally, with the physical act of love—almost succeeded in breaking down that high, carefully constructed wall she'd built about herself.

But she'd repulsed him, kept him at bay, and surely, if she could withstand a man so attractive and so ruthlessly determined as Nick, then she need fear no one . . . And yet wasn't the real danger right here within herself—the enemy within the gates?

Oh, she was being ridiculous. Would the real Carly Sheppard please stand up? And not that wanton stranger who had almost taken her over in a moment of madness in the conservatory.

She went through to the sitting-room and began prowling around it, picking up her favourite pieces of china, setting them down again and finally rearranging all her paperweights in their glass prison. There was a smear on one of them. She breathed on the frosty glass, then rubbed it with her handkerchief until it shone, then finally put it back down and reclosed the cabinet.

'I'm happy,' she said aloud, and from all round the room, it seemed to her as though her beloved possessions echoed her words. 'He's wrong—I *am* happy,' she declared fiercely, and went back to the kitchen to begin the unpacking.

CHAPTER EIGHT

'THIS isn't the way back, surely?'

Lost in her own thoughts, Carly had not registered Nick turning off the main road, but now she realised that they were climbing steadily along narrow lanes, with the bleak hillsides beyond.

'It's quieter this way. And anyway, I fancied a run across the moors. No objections, I trust?'

'N-no,' she said hastily, unnerved by the faint note of irritation in Nick's voice. 'That's great.'

'Good.' And still looking straight ahead, he relapsed into the morose silence he had maintained ever since they had left the trade symposium in Harrogate.

Carly expelled her breath in a silent little puff and turned her head to study the passing stone walls and fells. He'd been like this for nearly four weeks now. Edgy—no, more than edgy; he was tetchy, short-tempered, moody—you name it, he was it, she thought despondently.

That Monday after their disastrous weekend, she had climbed the stairs to his office with even greater trepidation than on her very first morning, fearful of how he'd greet her. But in the event he had not made even the most oblique reference to the previous day, and it had stayed that way, with him being merely decidedly cool with her—and edgy.

And she hadn't been the only one to be on the receiving end of his tongue, either. At lunchtime yesterday, the latest in what was developing into a long line of very temporary secretaries had fled in tears. Carly had been strongly tempted to join her, but she was determined to stick this shadowing out, if only not to give Nick the satisfaction of seeming to turn tail and run away from him.

But now at last, thank heaven, it was the final Tuesday of term, and after today she wouldn't see him until January. Perhaps three weeks without her enforced company—plus liberal helpings of turkey and Christmas pudding, she added ironically—might just sweeten that temper of his.

They were approaching a village, the grey millstone of the cottages making it look as though it was growing up the steep hillside. Carly caught sight of the white place name beside the road and gave a gasp of astonishment.

'*Haworth!*' She turned to Nick, her eyes glowing with delight. 'How wonderful!'

'Mmm,' he grunted as he swung the Aston Martin through a car park entrance.

'Oh, thank you!'

'Well, it's about time you got here.' There was still that note of asperity in his voice. 'And you've shown very little sign of ever making it under your own steam.'

Carly stared at his forbidding profile as he pulled into a parking space, but said nothing.

'Out you get,' he ordered.

'No,' she said tightly. 'You've brought me here—OK, but you've spoilt it for me before we even arrive. So I won't bother, thanks all the same.'

Leaning past her, he clicked open her door. 'Out!'

For a second, Carly pushed herself further back in her seat. But then she really did desperately want to see the Parsonage where the Brontë sisters had lived and died... And besides, Nick had already got out and was advancing on her side of the car, with the obvious intention of dragging her out by the hair if she didn't co-operate.

She clambered out and followed him up a short flight of steps and across the narrow cobbled street towards the stark outline of the house. The glow inside her had quite gone, but she told herself fiercely, I won't let him spoil it for me, I won't. And, going ahead of him, she pushed open the gate in the wall, walked through the small garden, then, her heart beating a little tattoo of excitement, up the steps to the front door.

Nick caught up with her in the entrance hall and as she looked up at him he slanted her a funny little half-smile. If I didn't know you better, she thought, I might have imagined that there was a hint of apology in those sapphire eyes.

On the left of the stone-flagged passage was the sitting-room. They stood in the doorway looking in, and her first reaction was complete disbelief. This was such a very ordinary room—fireplace, ornaments, curtains—and yet, in here, the three sisters had sat every evening scribbling out the books which would make Haworth and this house a shrine for pilgrims from all around the world.

And there, against the wall, was the very sofa on which Emily had died. Carly stared at it, remembering how Charlotte had described to her friend Elizabeth Gaskell how she'd searched everywhere for a last withered spray of heather to bring home to her dying sister, to remind her of her beloved moors. And then the letter, just a few days later. 'There is no Emily in time or on earth now...the anguish of seeing her suffer is over.' Carly felt a hard knot tighten on her throat and, biting her lip, turned away.

Upstairs were more poignant reminders: Emily's white and gold christening mug, Charlotte's clothes—a pretty bonnet, a pair of boots...the tiny books, hardly larger than postage stamps, written when they were children...the brass collar of Emily's bull mastiff, Keeper, who had walked alongside her coffin through the churchyard, stayed all through the funeral service, then lay down outside his mistress's bedroom and howled for days...

'All right?' Nick was looking at her closely.

'Yes.' She gave a rather shaky laugh. 'It's just that it all seems so near, doesn't it? I mean, Charlotte got dressed in her white muslin in this very room to go down that path there,' she pointed out of the window, 'to the church to marry Mr Nicholls. And then, just a few months later, she was carried back to the church. What did she say just before she died? Oh yes—"I am not going to die, am I? We have been so happy."' Her voice choked into silence.

'Hmm.' Nick regarded her thoughtfully. 'You know, I would never have thought that the poised, self-assured Miss Caroline Sheppard could be such a little sentimentalist.'

'I'm not,' she replied indignantly. 'It's just that on a dark December day like this, with hardly anyone else about, it's so easy to imagine it all, somehow. Anyway,' she gave him a radiant smile, 'I'm so glad I've been. Thank you, Nick.'

But instead of returning her smile he only said brusquely, 'Well, if you've seen everything you want, we'll get on.' And he turned on his heel, leaving her to follow.

He did not wait while she looked around the gift shop and was standing impatiently by the car when she got back to it, clutching a carrier bag of souvenirs. As she came up to him, her eyes widened in astonishment when she saw that he had changed into walking boots.

'We've got time for a walk,' he announced curtly.

'A walk?' Carly echoed with a sinking heart. 'But I've only got these.' And she held out one slim foot encased in a high-heeled black pump.

He thrust some red woollen socks and a pair of elegant suede and leather fell boots at her.

'Put these on. They should fit you—they're Simone's.' Her head jerked up and just for a moment their eyes held, an awareness in each of the same unspoken memory.

'She only wore them once, though,' he went on, ironically, 'before she decided that walking the Pennine Way was definitely not her scene.'

'But where are we going? Not that I *mind*,' Carly added hastily, not wishing to be put on a level with his maligned sister-in-law.

'I thought we'd go to Top Withens.'

'The old farmhouse that Emily used as Wuthering Heights? Oh, yes, I'd love to.'

As she dropped her shoes into the car boot beside Nick's, she saw a shiny black wet suit, a helmet with a powerful-looking lamp attached and a coil of rope.

'Is that your potholing gear?' she asked.

'Yes. I went over to Ingleton on Sunday and haven't got around to clearing it out of the car yet. Ready?'

They walked up behind the Parsonage and through a meadow crossed by a line of stepping stones. Coming towards them was another pair of walkers, but these were really dressed for the part in anoraks and over-trousers, sweat-bands on their foreheads in spite of the cold wind, and weighed down by huge rucksacks.

As they met, she and Nick were on the receiving end of a pair of very superior looks, and glancing down, she could see why, with her boots and red socks combined with a navy business suit and neat polka-dot blouse, and

Nick in a charcoal grey suit, the trousers tucked into his bright blue socks.

Her lips twitched and she tried to catch his eye, but he seemed totally oblivious to her amusement, doggedly looking straight ahead. Just a few weeks ago, she thought sadly, as she struggled to keep up with his long strides, they would have shared the joke, both of them dissolving into easy laughter. But not now...

At the far end of the field was a stone stile. Nick went over it first, and, as she was following, her foot caught on the top rung. She overbalanced and as he instinctively put up his arms she fell neatly into them. Just for a moment she lay, winded, against his chest.

'Sorry.' She looked up at him, but without even a glance at her he dumped her on her feet, as though she were a distasteful burden he wished to be rid of, and strode on.

'What did you buy in the shop?' They were out on the open moor now, and his voice broke a long silence.

'Some cologne for myself, a pack of Christmas cards with the Parsonage on them. Oh, and some last-minute gifts—small ones to put on the Christmas tree at home.'

'So you're going to your parents for Christmas?'

'Yes.' Carly wrinkled her nose slightly. 'Term ends on Thursday and I'm going to them on Friday.'

'You don't sound very keen.' Nick turned to shoot her a glance.

'Well, it's my first Christmas at the cottage and I'd really have preferred to stay up here. But—well, you know, Christmas. What are you doing?'

'Oh, I'm off to Guildford,' he said grimly. 'I'm driving my father down. Well, he obviously wants to see Nicky. He's his only grandchild—and likely to remain so,' he added drily. 'I don't suppose Simone has any intention of letting that particular catastrophe happen again.'

'But what about you? I mean——' Appalled, Carly blundered into silence, feeling the colour zing into her cheeks.

'To provide him with a few more grandchildren, you mean?' he asked laconically. 'No, I imagine that's even less likely, Carly.'

'Oh.' She cleared her throat. 'Are we nearly there?'

'Yes. Top Withens is just ahead, up there at the top of this rise.'

'But it's a *ruin*!' Carly wailed a few minutes later, as she surveyed the tumbledown stone house beside the track.

'But don't you prefer it this way?' There was an ironic glint in his eye. 'It's much more romantic, surely.'

He hunkered down on a grassy mound, his back against a stunted hawthorn bush, and after a moment's hesitation, she joined him. The low winter sun had emerged briefly from behind some leaden clouds, and it was almost warm out of the keen wind.

All around them, the moors rolled away to the skyline, bleak and inhospitable. Imagine being lost out here. 'Let me in—let me in. I'm come home. I'd lost my way on the moor...' The ghostly Catherine's voice echoed in her ear, as the wind rustled the dry hawthorn branches, and Carly shivered.

'Are you cold?' Nick, who seemed to have been caught up in his own brooding thoughts, glanced briefly at her. 'Do you want to go back?'

'Oh, no, not yet,' she said hurriedly. 'It's just that it's so forbidding out here. Are there any potholes?'

'Not as far as I'm aware of.'

'Why do you like it—potholing—so much?' she asked curiously.

He shrugged. 'Why not?'

'Well——' she pondered '—I can understand anyone enjoying gliding, or water-skiing, or even parachuting. But going down under the ground, squeezing along dark holes, diving into subterranean rivers—horrible! And it's so dangerous.'

'It's not that dangerous—not if you know what you're doing. But I suppose it's precisely because there is an element of risk.' Nick pursed his lips in thought. 'Every time I go down a pot, even one I know well, it's a challenge. And with my build, it makes it more—well, tricky.'

Carly shuddered involuntarily at the image of Nick struggling through a narrow fissure in the rock, maybe, in spite of all his precautions, getting stuck, hundreds of feet underground...

'Besides,' he went on, 'there's always the thrill, the chance that you'll be the first to break through into a new cave system. But with more people doing it, it gets harder all the time, so you have to go deeper, take more chances, perhaps.' He grinned at her. 'I'm quite determined that one day I'll be the first into a new system, though. Imagine, the world-famous Bradley Cavern—you'll be able to tell your grandchildren that you knew the great Nick Bradley.'

Before she could respond, he continued, 'Anyway, that's how I get my kicks. Setting off on each dive, positive that one day I really will be the first through that rock, under that river.'

'Tell me,' her voice was tight, 'is there anything you do badly?'

Nick got to his feet. 'Only lose,' he said softly, looking down at her, his face as bleak as the moor around them. 'I lose very badly, Carly.'

He turned away and went across to the ruined house, peering through a crack in the doorway.

'Come and see.'

He turned back towards her, the setting sun lighting him up against the grey stone wall, and suddenly—keyed up as she was—the thought struck her like a blow. Of course. Heathcliff. How had she not seen it—that likeness—before? One man the fiction of Emily Brontë's brain; the other warm, alive, in front of her. And yet...both dark, both saturnine—and both exuding a ruthless determination to achieve their goals, not to be thwarted in any way...

The sun disappeared behind the threatening clouds, and she shivered again at the sudden chill.

Carly rolled over with a groan. Opening her eyes, she tried to sit up, but that was a dreadful mistake; the whole wall—in fact, the whole room—was gyrating slowly around her. She closed her eyes again and fell back on the pillow.

'It's just a bit of a chill,' she'd told her mother on the phone. 'I got wet a couple of days ago.' And that was an understatement. Halfway back from Top Withens, the skies had opened and by the time they reached the car she had been soaked, while Nick who, in spite of all her protestations, had taken off his jacket and enfolded her in it, was if possible even wetter.

'Anyway, Mummy, you're not to come up.'

'Well, if you're quite sure, darling.' Behind the reluctance she had sensed the relief. 'We've got that party here on Christmas Eve, and then the Hunt are coming as usual for a buffet lunch on Boxing Day, so it would be rather——'

Mrs Sheppard's voice had tailed away and Carly, wincing as another vicious stab of pain shot through her head, said, 'Now, you're not to worry. I'll be fine. Love to Dad—have a good Christmas.'

And she'd put the receiver down and tottered upstairs, clutching a hot water bottle. That had been—how long ago had it been? She moved her head restlessly on the crumpled pillow, trying to clear her confused mind, gave up and drifted off into an uneasy doze, to wake from that with a violent start, to toss, turn, doze and wake again.

Very gingerly, she tried opening one eye again, and this time the room lurched but then stayed in place. Her head was thumping, every muscle—no, every particle of her body ached as though she'd been kicked by a horse.

How could getting wet make her feel like this? It was all his fault—if he hadn't dragged her halfway across those horrible moors, she'd be safe at home now...

Anyway, she couldn't lie here forever—though nobody would care if she did. She sniffed and a couple of weak tears filled her eyes and overflowed. Oh, come on, no self-pity, please, she thought. Then, If only my head would stop aching, if only I could just get a cup of tea...

As she swung her legs over the edge of the bed, the room tilted again, but she managed to feel for her dressing-gown and ease herself into it. While she'd slept, someone had changed the stuffing in her body for cotton wool, and her teeth were chattering violently. The room was freezing cold. Of course—she'd programmed the central heating boiler just to tick over while she was away.

The stairs were a problem; her legs had turned to badly set jelly and the pink tweed carpet had changed into a roller-coaster. But at last, clinging to the banister, she got safely to the bottom.

The kitchen, when she pushed open the door, was a white dazzle. She put up her hand to shield her sore eyes and saw that there was a light sprinkling of snow on the trees outside. A white Christmas.

If only her head would stop this terrible pounding! It was shaking her, making the entire room vibrate. She put her hands to her ears, pressing them hard, then finally registered what she would have known far sooner if she had not been so dazed. The banging was not coming from inside her—it was from outside. As she stared at the door, she saw with a flicker of fear a dark shadow, which blotted out the light from the tiny window beside it. Someone was out there.

Tentatively, she opened the door, and for a moment pure joy overwhelmed her as she saw Nick, crouched among the lower branches of the pear tree, hammering frantically at the wall. But she was delirious, she had to be. This was a different Nick—one who had sprouted Dracula-like fangs from his mouth.

Nick/Dracula caught sight of her, started violently, clutched at his mouth, then spat out into his hand the nails he'd been holding between his teeth.

'Carly? What on earth——?' Then, '*Carly*!' He leapt to his feet, flinging down the hammer. 'Are you all right?'

'Of course I am.'

Feebly she tried to push him away, but then, as she began to fold into a neat heap at his feet, she felt him catch her up in his arms, and with a little sigh she let go.

CHAPTER NINE

WHEN she came to, she was lying in bed and Nick was sitting beside her, regarding her grimly. As she tried to sit up, he put out a hand and pushed her back down.

'You stay right there.'

'No,' she muttered, 'I-I'm all right. It's just a slight chill.'

'Mmm.' He pursed his lips. 'Was there any flu about in school at the end of term?'

'Yes, quite a lot. Oh, no!' Carly gave a groan. Flu. Of course, that would explain the dreadful ache, the intense weakness that was turning her body to water.

Nick reached across and laid a cool hand on her brow, his touch as impersonal as a stranger's.

'You're like fire. What the hell were you playing at, getting out of bed like that?' He stood up, smoothing the duvet up to her chin. 'I'll get you a drink. Tea?'

'Please.' And she buried her nose in the pillow as a flood of weak tears threatened.

She could dimly hear him moving about downstairs in the kitchen, and before she had time to more than begin to think that she rather liked the idea of him down there, he was back.

Opening the cover a fraction, he slid a hot water bottle down beside her, then, as she tried to raise herself, he put his hands under her arms and drew her up gently, holding her while he arranged the pillows, then laying her against them. But once again, he did all this with a brisk, impersonal efficiency which almost repelled her.

'I did the tea in a mug. I thought you'd manage it better—or do you want me to hold it for you?'

'No—no, I can manage.'

Hastily she took the mug from him and cradled its warmth between her fingers, then took a scalding sip.

'Oh, marvellous! Thank you.' She smiled up at him, but he did not return her smile.

'Will you be all right now if I go?'

Across the rim of the mug she stared at him, her eyes widening. He was leaving her. She knew she ought to say, Yes, I'm fine. You go on—don't let me detain you a minute longer. But instead she felt her mouth turn down at the corners and next moment a loud sob burst out.

'What the——?'

Nick gazed down at her in total astonishment for a moment, then, taking the mug from her shaking hands, he plumped down on the bed and dragged her to him.

'Carly, whatever's the matter?'

'Nothing. It's just the flu.' She snuffled against his chest, then, horrified, heard herself say, on a hiccup, 'And you're leaving me.'

Under his cheek, she felt a laugh which was hastily smothered, then he said, 'But I'm not going for good. All I'm doing is nipping back home to get my things.'

'Your—things?'

'Yes. And then I'm coming straight back here to look after you.'

This was even worse. He couldn't possibly look after her. 'No, I'll——'

'Shut up,' he said amicably. He held her away from him, took out a folded handkerchief from his trouser pocket and wiped her wet face as though she were a baby. 'Now, drink your tea like a good girl, and by the time you've had a little sleep I'll be back.'

Carly drank greedily as he watched her, then handed him the mug.

'How long have you been like this?' he asked.

'Oh, I don't know. I just lost touch with time.' She frowned in the effort to focus her fuddled brain. 'What day is it?'

'Boxing Day.'

'Boxing Day? Oh, lord.' She fell back on her pillow, pulling a rueful face. 'Whatever happened to Christmas?'

As Nick reached the door, through the waves of sleep which were reaching out to engulf her, her mind caught at something. 'What were you doing outside?'

But he only grinned. 'All will be revealed. Now, go to sleep.'

As the front door softly closed Carly thought drowsily, Nick's in Guildford. I must have been hallucinating. But the tang of his citrus aftershave still hung in the air and, smelling it, she drifted off to sleep with a little smile on her face.

When she half roused, aching and sweaty, it was dark outside. She turned her head against the pillow, muttering to herself, then through her stupor felt a pair of arms lift her so that she was supported against something firm and solid.

'Drink this, Carly.' A glass of lemon barley water was held to her parched lips and she gulped it down, then the arms laid her back, her clammy forehead was gently wiped with a cold cloth, and the same soft voice, which she knew she ought to recognise, whispered, 'Now go to sleep. I'll be here if you need me.' And, obedient as a child, she turned over and fell into another fitful doze.

When she finally woke, daylight was filtering in through the closed curtains and, though she was weak still, that dreadful light-headedness had gone. But surely, through that long night, someone had been there—a pair of comforting, caring hands...She struggled to remember, but then, as she rolled over on to her other side, she froze.

Sprawled uncomfortably in her dainty Victorian tub chair, a blanket over him, was Nick, his head cushioned against one hand, sound asleep. His white shirt was unbuttoned and he badly needed a shave. She stared across at him, conscious of his soft, regular breathing, and as she stared, strange, disquieting emotions began to jangle discordantly inside her.

As though sensing her eyes on him, he came to, catlike, instantly wide awake. He gave her a faint smile. 'Feeling better?'

'Mmm.' She nodded weakly. 'Were you here—all night?'

He pushed the blanket away and got up, stretching himself gingerly. 'That's right.' He perched on the bed and put his hand on her brow. 'Good—your temperature's down nicely.'

The touch of him, the faint smell of sweat, the feel of his body, trapping her leg against the sheet, were all intensely disturbing to her and, conscious suddenly that she was dressed only in a flimsy nightdress, she shrank down a little under the duvet.

'Thank you, Nick, for staying with me.' She did not quite look at him. 'It was very kind of you, but I'm fine now.'

He raised one black brow. 'And so I'm to go off and leave you, I suppose.'

'Yes. I-I shall be all right now.' Though deep down she wasn't at all sure that she would be.

'Certainly not—and no arguing.' He stood up, running his hand across his chin. 'I'll go and have a shower and a shave, though, if I may—although I seem to remember you telling me once how much you admired my macho whiskers.' He shot her a provocative look, but Carly, still several degrees under, only buried her nose deeper beneath the coverlet. 'And then I'll get us something to eat.'

'Oh no, please—just a cold drink for me.' But he had gone.

She could hear him moving about in the bathroom, then the whine of his electric razor. She lay there, listening idly to the sounds, then thought suddenly how comforting it was to have him there. He must be having a shower now, the water was gushing down. He'd be in her frosted glass cubicle, the hot water sluicing over his head and shoulders as he soaped that strong body, the droplets gleaming on the silky, tanned skin——

As the potent images took shape in her mind, a tidal wave of heat engulfed her so that she could feel sweat bursting out all over her and, hastily flinging herself over into a cooler part of the bed, she concentrated all her attention on a male blackbird which was stridently proclaiming his territory on the pear branch just outside her window. Another imperious, self-assertive male, she thought with wry amusement, and drifted off to sleep again.

She was disturbed when Nick, his curls still damp but clean-shaven and smelling of soap, came in carrying a loaded tray.

'But I told you—only a drink,' she protested feebly.

'I know you did—and I've got you this. It's only orange juice, plus a poached egg on toast, and you're going to eat it, if I have to force-feed you with every mouthful.'

As she slid reluctantly upright, all too conscious now of her shoulders, bare apart from the narrow straps, and her upper breasts, only partly hidden by the white lace inserts of her nightdress, he said brusquely, 'Have you got a bedjacket or something?'

'I think it's in that drawer.'

'This'll do.'

He picked up the pale blue sweater he had obviously shed during the night and draped it round her shoulders. The soft cashmere of the sleeves brushed gently against her neck, enfolding her in their warmth as though in his arms, and, ridiculously, she felt more tears spring to her eyes.

'What's wrong now?' Nick, knife and fork poised, was eyeing her.

'Oh, nothing. Just the usual post-flu sag, I suppose.' She managed a feeble smile and began on her poached egg.

'I presume you managed to tell your parents you couldn't make it for Christmas?' he asked.

'Oh, yes. It's just as well it came on before I set out. I'd hate to have collapsed halfway down the motorway.' Carly sighed. 'If I'm well enough, I'll have to try to get down for New Year. Anyway, what about you? I thought you were in Guildford.'

'I was.' He gave a grimace. 'But a little family life with Martin and Simone goes quite a long way. I came back early yesterday morning—a great journey, nothing on the roads.'

'But did your father want to leave so soon?'

'Martin's bringing him back next week.' A smile of almost feminine tenderness softened his hard-edged face. 'I left him playing with the electric train set I bought for Nicky.'

'I like your father—very much,' Carly said suddenly.

'Just a pity about his elder son, I suppose.' Nick slanted her a curious little smile, but then went on, 'The feeling's mutual, actually. He thinks you're great. In fact, he——'

He broke off, collecting up the dirty dishes, and though she looked up at him expectantly he did not finish the sentence.

'But I suppose you'd have been coming back in a day or so, in any case,' Carly pointed out. 'To open up the foundry, I mean.'

But while she was trying to maintain a semblance of normal conversation, to her horror she found herself becoming increasingly aware that quite a large part of her mind was busy deciding just how pleased she was that he'd come back early, that she positively *liked* having him around, that the small, neat cottage was somehow warmer, more complete with a large, masculine presence padding around in it. But it was a part of her that she had to stamp on—hard.

'So you'll have to leave me soon, anyway,' she added.

Nick gave her a long look. 'Sorry to disappoint you, but we're closed until after the New Year. We used to open, but I won't have men with hangovers handling molten metal, so now we stay closed. I do have an appointment in Bristol on the thirty-first——'

'Well, there you are, then.'

'—but I'll cancel that, if necessary. So, you ungrateful young woman, you're stuck with me. Now,' he said as he stood up, 'if you behave yourself and have a good sleep, I *may* let you get up for a while this evening.'

'Bully!' Carly flung at him, then lay listening to his footsteps going downstairs before drifting off yet again, this time into a deep, untroubled sleep.

It was late afternoon when she finally roused and Nick helped her out of bed.

'Whoops! Sorry.' She clutched at him as her knees sagged, and he held her briefly—she couldn't help noticing how briefly—then sat her down on the edge of the bed while he wrapped her in her dressing-gown and a rug, then scooped her up in his arms and carried her downstairs, setting her in one of the armchairs in the sitting-room.

Outside, it was dark, but she could just see the light sprinkling of frozen snow which still lay on the lawn and coated every iron-hard bush. She shivered, but then he closed the curtains, switched on the wall lamps and the lights of her Christmas tree, and they were enclosed in a cosy circle of soft pink warmth.

'I like your tree. Just a pity it's a bit on the uneven side.'

Carly laughed. 'I wasn't going to bother, with going home, but I was in the market at the weekend and one of the traders pushed it at me, going cheap. It looked so pathetic with those broken branches that I couldn't resist it, so I bought the fairy lights and a few decorations—oh, I forgot,' she sat up abruptly, 'I put the presents I had from 5S underneath it and I haven't opened them yet.'

'In that case, perhaps it's about time you did.'

His tone was dry and for a second their eyes met, then slid apart. It's still there, between us, thought Carly, with a lurch of her insides—that terrible scene in the conservatory, the cruel things Nick had hurled at her, they hadn't gone at all. Beneath his caring for her and her gratefulness to him, that minefield still lay, just submerged, but waiting some time, somewhere, to explode in their faces.

'Here you are.' Nick dropped them into her lap and, with lowered eyes, she began to tug at the tinsel string of the first packet. 'Thank you for your scarf, by the way.'

'Oh.' She shrugged slightly. 'I hope you like it. I-I wasn't really sure what to buy you.'

In fact, given the level their relationship had sunk to, she hadn't been sure whether it would be right to buy him a present at all, but in the end she had settled for an expensive and certainly tasteful—but totally safe— navy mohair scarf.

She deliberately left until last the small silver-wrapped package which he had thrust into her hands when he dropped her off after their return from Haworth. 'Don't open it until Christmas,' he'd ordered, and all that evening, as she'd alternately shivered and coughed, her eyes had strayed back to that tiny parcel.

Now, rather self-conscious under his scrutiny, she pulled back the paper and lifted the lid of the white box. She moved aside the cotton wool, then stared down at the contents.

'Oh!' She breathed a long sigh. 'Thank you!'

She looked up at him, her eyes shining, but he just said, 'I hope you haven't got one like it already.'

'Oh, no. It's *beautiful*!'

Carefully she took out the glass paperweight and held it up, the Christmas tree lights reflecting tiny coloured prisms in its dome. At the centre, a young girl, her fair hair streaming in the frozen wind, stood on tiptoe, her face alight as she caught a white feather that had fallen from a line of geese which flew overhead.

'It's Victorian, isn't it?' she said.

'Yes. I saw it in the antiques mall in town a few weeks ago.'

She wanted to ask him, Did you get it *before*—or after? But the words stuck fast in her throat and he went on casually, 'I thought the girl looked a bit like you.'

'Oh.' She stared at him, then hastily looked back at the paperweight. 'It's—it's wonderful, Nick.'

Her voice choked into silence and he said quickly, 'Hey, no tears—or I'll have it back!' As she tried to laugh, he went down on his haunches and, with the tip of his finger, flicked away the tear which trembled on her lashes.

'Shall I put it in the cabinet for you?'

'Yes, please.'

She watched as he carefully made room for it. How delicate and precise his touch was for such a large man. Well, you knew that already, didn't you? that inner voice which had been silent for days suddenly whispered in her ear. Those hands were every bit as delicate and precise that day, when you were——

Her whole body jerked under the spasm of nervous tension that shook her, and to cover it she said, 'Can we watch TV? It's *The Sound of Music*, I think.'

Nick pulled a face. 'For the five hundred and fiftieth Christmas running.'

She laughed. 'Please—I do like it.'

But in fact, quite a while before Maria walked down the aisle to marry her handsome baron, Carly had been caught out unsuccessfully trying to smother one yawn too many and, in spite of her sleepy protestations, been carried back upstairs and tucked into bed, exactly as though she were a child.

CHAPTER TEN

THREE mornings later, after being cosseted and indulged like a sickly Siamese kitten, Carly woke feeling almost her old self. Certainly, she was well enough to thoroughly enjoy the belated Christmas lunch Nick had prepared—although, by his own admission, the turkey portions and plum pudding had come from the mass of provisions laid in by his housekeeper to greet him on his return from Guildford.

Afterwards, she insisted on helping him with the washing-up and then leaned against the unit, basking in the brilliant sunshine that streamed in through the window.

'Can we go out for a walk?' she asked him. 'I'm sure I'm well enough.'

'Hmm, well, perhaps——'

'Great. I'll get my jacket.'

'And a hat.'

'Oh—yes, sir.' She gave him a smart salute, then fled as he made a mock-threatening move towards her.

When she came back downstairs Nick, in jeans, his chunky Aran sweater and the new navy scarf, was already waiting, so she slipped her jacket on over her white lambswool sweater and black ski pants.

'Right, I'm ready.'

'Not quite, you're not.'

Catching up the pink woolly hat she was swinging by its pom-pom, he jammed it down over her ears, before winding the matching scarf tightly round her mouth, successfully muffling her protests.

Then, as though on impulse, he dropped a light kiss neatly between her eyebrows. If it had been an impulse, he obviously regretted it immediately, for his lips had barely brushed her skin before he was drawing back, turning to lead the way out of the cottage and leaving Carly, her brow still tingling faintly, to follow.

He took the path which struck up on to the moor and soon she was labouring behind him, gasping for breath. He waited for her at the top of the rise, shoulders hunched, hands jammed into his trouser pockets, and as she came slowly up to him she saw that his face was very sombre.

'You're tired,' he said curtly. 'We'd better go back.'

'Oh, no!' She caught at his arm imploringly. 'I'm not—honestly. I just got a bit out of breath on that slope. But it's doing me good. I mean—just look at that!' Her arm took in the wide, majestic sweep of moorland running up to some jagged crags, their snowy summits outlined against the blue sky, and she turned to him, her face glowing. 'Isn't it wonderful?'

As he stared down at her, a skylark broke from almost at their feet and soared upwards, filling the air with its bubbling song. The hard lines of his face softened and he smiled.

'Yes, it is.' He seemed to shake off whatever black dog had been crouched across his shoulders and caught at her hand. 'Come on, I'll help you.' And instantly he was transformed into a happy, laughing companion.

The sun was low in the sky when they reluctantly turned for home. The air was like champagne and Carly felt her spirits fizzing. They were almost back at the cottage when she saw, in the lee of a clump of boulders, a heap of powdery snow. Nick was a few paces ahead and, ramming some of the snow into a ball, she took aim and hurled it.

As it splattered on to the back of his neck, he spun round. 'Why, you little madam!'

He made a lunge for her and with a squeal of terror she ducked past him, down the last few yards of track and up her path. By the front door, though, she skidded to a halt and stood gazing, her hazel eyes wide.

'Oh, Nick! I didn't see it when we went out.'

'You like it? I intended it as a surprise for when you got back after Christmas—I had the surprise, though, when you opened the door on me.'

With her finger, Carly traced the small cast-iron oval on the wall. It was black, with a raised gold band around the edge, and the words 'Pear Tree Cottage' enamelled in white relief. Beside them was a tiny, perfect replica of a pear tree.

'It's—it's a *Doyenne du Comice*,' she said huskily, her finger resting on the squat, browny-gold fruit. 'It isn't just any pear tree—it's this one.' She gestured towards the gnarled old branches alongside the plaque.

'I'm glad it's recognisable.' Nick pulled a wry face. 'I had to check it out in a gardening book. A couple of years ago, we developed quite a good line in these personalised house names and I modified one of the moulds.'

'But you—you shouldn't have. You bought me the paperweight,' she said slowly, her eyes still on that delicate iron oval.

'Yes, well, if I'd known you were a demon marksman I wouldn't have done, of course.' He hooked a piece of melting snow from the neck of his sweater. 'But it's not an extra Christmas present—more a belated thank you

for putting up with my moods on Mondays and Tuesdays
without complaint—and yes,' he shot her a rueful smile,
'unbelievable as it may be, this is an oblique apology
for my bad temper these last few weeks. I'll try my best
not to be quite such a bear with a sore head from now
on.'

The words on the plaque were dancing up and down
through a shimmer of tears and Carly, her heart full to
bursting, turned her eyes up to his.

'Oh, Nick—it's the most beautiful name-plate ever.
Thank you!' And before rational thought could inter-
vene, she flung her arms round him and kissed his cheek.

But next moment, her euphoria was shattered. As
though her touch had burnt him Nick recoiled, brushing
her arms roughly away so that, with a little gasp of ice-
cold shock, she let them fall limply by her sides.

Blindly she pushed past him, fumbled the key into the
lock and jerked open the door. She took off her hat and
jacket, then went through to the sitting-room. The fire,
which Nick had lit earlier, had burned low, so she knelt
on the sheepskin rug in front of it and took up the brass
poker.

'Leave it.' He was standing in the doorway. 'We could
toast muffins on that. I noticed a pack in your freezer
this morning.'

Muffins toasted at an open fire—with all that that
conjured up of a warm, cosy togetherness? Was she
strong enough to bear that?

'If you like.' She did not look at him.

'Right, I'll fetch them.'

'No, you've waited on me quite enough.' She even
managed a faint smile. 'You stay here and I'll organise
it.'

When she carried in the tray Nick was seated on the sofa, his legs as usual stretched in front of him, scowling at the toecaps of his trainers. So much for his good intentions. Carly sighed inwardly, then knelt down on the rug and jabbed the prongs of the toasting fork into a muffin half. She thought at first that he was not going to move, but then he squatted down beside her,

'I've only got one proper toasting fork,' she said brightly. 'I'll toast them, and you can butter them and spread the honey if you like.'

He grunted something that just might have been 'Yes', and so when the first muffin was ready she tapped it off on to a plate and pushed it across to him. If someone were to look in through the window, she thought sadly, what would they see? A man and a woman, toasting muffins before an open fire, for all the world as if they were a happily——

'I think you're well enough now to be left, don't you?'

'What?' She stared round at him blankly.

'I said I think you're well enough,' he repeated, his voice crackling with irritability, 'to be left.' Then he added, as though to leave no possible room for misunderstanding, 'For me to go.'

'Tonight, you mean?' Carly faltered.

'Yes.' He neatly retrieved an overdone muffin and slid it from the prongs. 'And I think I'll be able to keep that appointment in Bristol tomorrow.'

'Y-yes.' Carly somehow pulled herself together. 'Of course you must go. I-I'm fine now.'

But she wasn't. A feeling of sadness—no, more than that, of tremendous desolation—was sweeping through her. She didn't want him to go—she wanted to be able to wake up in the morning and know that he was here, in the next room to hers, where he'd slept for the past three nights. It was so nice, so comforting to have Nick here—and she'd gladly put up with all his moodiness and ill-temper.

He mustn't go. She needed him, she wanted him—she ached for him. She glanced at him, his eyes dark in the firelight, the planes of his cheekbones softened in its glow, and even then, just for a moment, her mind, imprisoned for so long, still refused to make that final quantum leap. But then, the next second, she finally knew the truth. She yearned, with all her mind and body, to wake up tomorrow with Nick, not in the next room, but beside her in her bed, holding her in his arms.

But it was too late—he must be so certain of how she would react if he were to make another move towards her. It would have to come from her...

'Yes, Nick,' she said softly, 'I'm well enough now. But suppose I don't want you to go?'

She turned to face him and slowly put her hand on his, but he jerked it away.

'No, Carly! Don't be a damn fool.'

He was rejecting her poor, pathetic effort. Well, what else could she expect? Humiliated tears sprang to her eyes, she threw down the toasting fork and went to scramble to her feet. But her leg had gone to sleep under her and as a vicious jab of pins and needles shot through her she stumbled. Cannoning heavily into him, she knocked him off balance, and they went down together in a sprawling heap.

Nick, his face tight, caught her by the elbows and pushed her upright away from him, but recklessly she put out her hand and softly caressed his cheek.

'Carly?' he said huskily, but, overcome all at once by shyness, she bent her head, her lashes fluttering down

to conceal her expression. Gently he tilted her face upwards, forcing her to look at him.

'Carly?'

Still she could not speak, but he must have read her
answer in her eyes, for she heard his breath catch in his
throat. Then, as he reached for her, all at once the
tensions which for weeks had floated almost visibly in
the air between them like black specks of gunpowder
ignited into an explosion of passion.

For one long moment they stared into each other's
eyes as though feeding greedily on what they saw there,
then eyes were not enough. Clothes were shed, Carly
helping Nick remove hers, while at the same time
fumbling with the buttons of his shirt, pulling it down
until the firelight flickered on his magnificent silky brown
shoulders, then, as he twisted round to tug her from her
sweater, on his chest and the play of muscles across his
torso and belly.

She put her hand up and gently brushed the knuckles
across the crisp dark hairs, feeling the small points of
his nipples pucker and tighten under her skin. Then, with
a smothered half laugh, half growl of frustration, he
gave up the unequal struggle with the tiny pearl buttons
of her blouse. Putting up both hands, he wrenched it
apart from neckline to waist and dragged her clear of
it.

Dimly, she felt the catch of her bra go, then Nick was
cupping one of her breasts in his hands. Bending his
head, he encircled the throbbing centre with his mouth,
teasing the already taut nipple with his tongue and teeth
until Carly, shuddering with a need that left her faint
and dizzy, bit hard on her lip. Putting her damp palms
to his shoulders, she pulled him to her.

'Wait, my sweet.' His voice, harsh with desire, was barely recognisable.

Putting his hands to her waist, he pushed down, easing her ski pants and panties away from her. The blood was coagulating in her veins, thick with the fever that possessed her.

He knelt above her to unclasp the buckle of his jeans and slid out of them, kicking them away from him, then, as she reached up to take him in her arms, he came down on to her, his knee parting her thighs. She felt him tense, gather himself, then thrust forward.

'Oh, Nick!' With no more than a single, smothered gasp, she took him completely into herself.

He began to move within her, slowly, gently at first, until the rhythm caught her up too. Then, as she clung to him, her eyes wide but unseeing, he drove deeper and faster until for Carly there was nothing beyond the room, their two intertwined bodies and this powerful rhythm which, with every thrust, was inexorably driving her to discover some far place in herself which until now she had not known existed.

She ceased to breathe, her body stiffened, her nails tightened on his shoulders, and as a long, shuddering spasm racked his whole frame, she cried out again, a long, wordless cry, and they lay spent in each other's arms.

When, aeons later, Carly stirred, she put up her hand and brushed it softly across Nick's cheek. He captured it in his own, burying his lips in her palm.

'Carly?'

'Mmm?'

'Did I—hurt you?'

'A little. Just at first.'

'I was too rough with you.' His voice was filled with self-reproach. 'But I didn't realise you were a virgin.'

'Well, *thank* you. Whatever made you think I wasn't?' she asked ruefully.

'Oh, I don't know. Well, to be honest,' he went on, after an almost imperceptible pause, 'I'd worked out that the hang-ups you seemed to have in that way must go back to some bad sexual experience.'

'No,' she said tightly. 'Any—hang-ups I might have—well, they're not for that reason.' She couldn't say any more. She still wasn't ready to open all of her mind to Nick, not even now. One day, perhaps, but not now...

He raised himself on one elbow and regarded her sombrely, but, sensitive to her mood perhaps, did not probe her further. But still she needed to break the heaviness that was threatening to take them over.

'I suppose you're still planning on leaving me tonight?' she pouted.

He slanted her a sleek cat's smile. 'Beg me to stay.'

'I most certainly will not!'

'Well, you'll have to make it worth my while, then.' He smoothed the flat of his hand across her stomach, so that delicious tingles ran all through her body.

'But were you really going to go?' she persisted.

'Yes, I was, Carly—but for one reason, and one reason only, I promise you.' His eyes were following the trail of his fingers. 'If you only knew how hard it's been for me to keep my hands off you, these last few days especially—and I was quite sure that if I stayed here any longer—well...'

'And after the way I reacted last time?'

'That's right. And it seemed such a pity to risk breaking up such a beautiful friendship yet again.'

'Well, of course,' she murmured, shyly teasing, 'you did catch me at a weak moment, just getting over a nasty bout of flu.'

'And what's the best remedy for that, do you think?'

'Well,' she said ingenuously, 'they do say that if you've found a cure that works, all you need is the treatment as before.'

She leaned her head on his shoulder, so that Nick could gently rub his chin against her soft hair. Lifting one hand, she began tracing with her fingertips a pattern of delicate spirals all over his chest, then lower, across the firm muscles of his torso, and then, with her palm, over the sharp outline of his hip, the hard, utterly masculine lines of his body, for her such a fascinating contrast with her own softness.

'Maybe you shouldn't do that.' Nick's voice held a delicious menace that made her shiver.

'Oh, shouldn't I? Why not?'

She bent her head back to give him a look of wide-eyed innocence, then, as she felt the soft rumble of laughter from his chest, she deliberately raised her hand and ran it down his smooth flank again and across his stomach, revelling in the feel of the muscles tensing beneath the skin.

'I warned you. Come here, hussy,' Nick growled in her ear, then, turning her around, he pulled her down to him, her hair falling across his face.

The fierce edge of their passion had been sated a little in that first wild explosion which had shivered them into atoms. Gradually, though, as Nick's kisses deepened, sucking the honeyed sweetness of her mouth, his desire ignited once more and hers leapt to meet it, all her senses filled to overflowing with him.

She arched her neck against his hungry mouth, as he fastened on the crazily beating pulse at her throat, then slid on, over her engorged breasts and down the sweep of her stomach, to lick teasingly, tantalisingly around the cup of her navel, then lower still.

For a moment, Carly tensed and her fingers, which had been clutched convulsively in Nick's black curls, stilled, then she lay transfixed. Very softly, she began to tremble, as a sensation, almost shocking in its intensity, yet warm and golden and infinitely sweet, like summer and laughter and joy, unfolded into life very deep inside her.

This time, as he took her into his arms, holding her hips up to meet him, she yielded herself gladly to his first sure thrust. His heart thundered against her ribs as now the driving rhythm built instantly, hurtling them almost brutally out into some distant corner of the universe.

Nothing can ever be quite the same again. Lost in space, the thought flashed through her mind, and then together with Nick she tumbled back from infinity, through a shower of glittering meteorites, to earth. And I shall never be the same again.

Slowly, Nick raised his head from where it lay, inert, against her shoulder and gazed down at her, his eyes dark and warm.

'Nick,' she whispered.

'Carly.' His voice trembled slightly, and the smile he gave her was lopsided. 'My honey-sweet girl.'

With his teeth, he lifted a silky tress that lay across her face, then smiled again, this time more naturally. 'Your beautiful hair—how much I've longed to do this!'

A log fell in the grate, sending out a shower of dead ashes.

'The fire's out.' As he eased his warm body away from her, she murmured protestingly, shivering at the sudden chill. 'Come on, it's way past your bedtime.' He stood up, lifting her with him, then took her up into his arms.

Upstairs, cocooned beneath the duvet, he made love to her again, this time slowly, with heart-catching tenderness. Then at last he curled on his side, fitting her to him, and like a pair of drowsy animals they drifted into sleep.

CHAPTER ELEVEN

THE same blackbird, perched on the same pear tree branch, roused Carly next morning. She rolled over and came up hard against Nick's body. Opening her eyes, she saw him propped on one elbow, gazing down at her. Just for a moment, a wave of shyness swept through her—even after their night together she hadn't yet accustomed herself to being naked in front of him—but then she smiled, rather tremulously.

'What time is it?'

'No idea.' He inclined his head in the direction of the window. 'That wretched dawn chorus has been going on for hours, I know that.'

'Mmm. What shall we do today?'

'Well, I've got one or two ideas——' he slid her a wicked look that brought the colour to her cheeks '—for seeing the New Year in.'

'And what are they?' she asked demurely, but then, 'Oh, good heavens!' She sat bolt upright, clutching the duvet to her. 'Aren't you supposed to be going to Bristol today?'

'I was.' He lay back luxuriously, one hand behind his head. 'I'll ring and cancel it.'

'But was it important?'

'Fairly—a possible contract for one of the new developments in the Docks. But it'll have to wait.'

'Oh, no, Nick, you must go.'

He shook his head firmly. 'I'm not leaving you today.'

'I'll come with you, then.' ~~She~~ spoke on a sudden impulse. 'Bristol's lovely and I haven't been there for ages. I can look round Clifton or somewhere while you're at your meeting.'

'Hmm.' He sounded far from convinced. 'I can think of far better ways of spending the day, but all right,' he said reluctantly, then a fresh thought seemed to strike him. 'I tell you what, you said you ought to try and see your parents over the New Year—well, we can make a detour on the way back.'

'Oh, no, Nick!' Horrified at where her hasty tongue had taken her, Carly tried to backtrack. 'I-I'm not really sure I'm well enough to go that far.'

'Nonsense. And anyway, we must practically go past their front door.'

'But—but they'll be having a New Year's Eve party. They always do.'

'Even better. We can see the New Year in with them. Besides, it's time I met them, if only to thank them for producing such a gorgeous daughter.'

But she could not respond to his teasing smile and sat chewing her lip. Useless even to try and explain that she needed still to keep the two strands of her life separate, that she wasn't yet secure enough within herself to bring them together. One glance at Nick's face, though, was enough to tell her that further argument would be futile—his mind was made up.

'I'll go and ring them,' she said, and went to get out of bed.

'No hurry for that.' He caught hold of her hand. 'We don't need to leave for hours yet, I'm sure.'

Behind her a car horn gave an imperious blast and Carly turned, then seeing the red Aston Martin, waved and went towards it across the grass. But she found she could not walk—she had to run, and she went on running straight into Nick's arms.

He lifted her clean off the ground in a bear-hug. 'Miss me?'

'Certainly not—even though——' she made a little moue '—you've been gone nearly two hours.'

'Sorry, my sweet. Promise I shan't leave you again today.' He kissed her full on the mouth and for a moment she clung to him, before he set her down and opened the passenger door for her.

As he settled himself in beside her, she asked, 'How did it go?'

'Not sure.'

'Oh, yes, you are,' she laughed. 'You've got a smirk on your face like a cat that's had all the cream.'

His grin widened. 'Well, all right, then. It went brilliantly—another order in the bag.'

'Huh! Another sucker fallen headlong for the crafty Bradley technique, I suppose.'

'Like you, you mean.' Then, before she could come up with a suitable rejoinder to cut him down to size, he slid in the clutch and eased out into the line of slow-moving traffic.

'Oh, Nick,' Carly tried to suppress the faint flicker of unease as she caught sight of a sign to the motorway, 'I still wish we were going straight back to Milton.'

'Of course you don't. You know you're dying to show me off to your parents.'

'Nicholas Bradley, you are utterly impossible—do you know that?'

She gave him a playful punch in the ribs, then, catching the eye of the driver of a police patrol car alongside, hastily turned her head to admire the lovely old stone buildings of Bristol.

Nick craned to look out at the small village church they were passing, half hidden among the trees.

'I suppose you were a perfectly angelic little choirgirl there,' he said teasingly.

'Of course—until I picked a fight with the head choirboy and blacked his eye on the day the Bishop came.'

'What an awful child you must have been! I'm just grateful I didn't know you then.' But the smile he gave her warmed her down to her toes.

'We're nearly there,' she told him. 'You take the next turn on the left, after the Rectory.'

Nick swung the car into the turning and up the familiar drive, fringed with trees and shrubs, then out past a wide sweep of manicured lawn and up to the lovely, porticoed manor house, its honey-gold Cotswold stone glowing in the pale afternoon sunlight.

He slowed and gave a long, soft whistle. 'What a beautiful house!'

'Yes, it is, isn't it?' Carly said quietly, all the bubbling elation she had been feeling earlier quite evaporated.

Nick shook his head slowly. 'I don't know how you ever left such a glorious home.'

'Don't you?' She smiled brightly. 'Oh, look—there's Mummy.'

'Caroline, darling, how lovely to see you.' Mrs Sheppard, in a pale blue twin-set and blue tweed skirt, her still fair hair captured in an elegant pleat, put up a cool cheek for her daughter to kiss. 'Too tiresome that you should be unwell at Christmas!'

'Oh, but I'm fine again now, honestly.' Carly, aware of Nick standing beside her, went on, a shade self-consciously, 'Mummy, this is Nick—Nick Bradley.'

'Mr Bradley.' Her mother extended a polite hand, but her eyes, after one swift reconnoitre that took in the whole of Nick, were cold.

'Oh, please, do call me Nick,' he responded, and Carly, caught between the two, felt the chill ripple of mutual antipathy.

'You come from—Yorkshire, I believe,' her mother murmured, and Carly was torn between laughter and tears at the inflection in her voice, which subtly contrived to place Yorkshire somewhere between Siberia and Outer Mongolia.

'That's right, Mrs Sheppard—Yorkshire born and bred.' And this time she had to suppress a giggle as she registered that Nick had ever so slightly broadened his accent for his hostess's benefit.

'Shall we get the luggage inside?' she asked quickly and, seizing her weekend case, walked up the steps and into the hall.

Her mother led the way upstairs and paused at a bedroom door. 'This is the principal guest-room, Mr Br—Nick. I do hope you'll be comfortable.'

'I'm sure I shall, thank you, Mrs Sheppard.'

Superficial politeness—underneath, all glacial ice, thought Carly, her ears pricked for every nuance, then allowed herself to be led along the corridor by her mother.

'I've put you in your old room, darling.' She hesitated, then went on delicately, 'I prepared *separate* rooms, of course,' with a glance at her daughter which Carly could not quite meet.

'Of course,' she murmured, and walked into her bedroom, still furnished with the white furniture and pretty patchwork quilt-covered bed from her childhood.

Her mother followed her into the room. 'This man— you haven't told me about him. Until this morning on the telephone, that is.'

'Perhaps because there's nothing to tell,' Carly replied quietly.

'But, darling, you will be careful, won't you? Is it wise to get too involved with a man like him?'

With any man, surely? Carly bit back the words and instead said rapidly, 'But I told you I was having to do this shadowing, didn't I?'

Mrs Sheppard sighed. 'Yes, darling, you did. Though why ever you had to go up there——'

'Well, Nick owns the iron foundry where I work. I shadow him,' she said, and, ignoring her mother's sagging jaw, went on, 'Is Daddy here?'

'No.' Her mother's lips tightened. 'Your father's gone up to London.'

Carly's heart contracted in a faint echo of the old childish terror. 'But he'll be back in good time for the party, surely?'

'I certainly hope so.'

Carly gave her a quick hug. 'It's lovely to be home, Mummy. And now, I promised to show Nick the grounds before it gets dark.'

'You know something?' Nick broke a rather long silence, the only sound their footsteps scuffing on the paved terrace.

'What?' Carly tried to rouse herself from her thoughts.

'I've decided you're exactly like the countryside down here. Beautiful, well-groomed—and deliciously soft-centred.'

'Mmm?'

'Joke, my darling. Cue for you to say, "Well, you're exactly like a lump of millstone grit."' But when she still did not respond, he put an arm round her shoulders, his cheek against her hair. 'What is it, sweetie?'

'Oh, nothing.' She managed to flash him a rather frayed smile. 'Maybe I'm catching your moodiness the way I caught flu at school. Come on.' She seized hold of his hand. 'I'll show you the stables.'

'Do you ride?' Nick, his hands in his pockets, lounged against the wall watching her as she fed sugar lumps to Xerxes, her father's big black hunter.

'All gone, boy.' She gently scratched his glossy forehead, then turned to Nick. 'I used to—I always had a pony.'

'And you rode to hounds, I suppose.' He was strolling by her side.

'Well, not really. To be honest, it used to sicken me.' She pulled a face. 'I was a grave disappointment, I think—Dad used to be Master of the local hunt. I preferred taking my pony and riding out on the hills all day.'

'Alone?'

'Yes. Oh, it was quite safe.'

'That's not what I meant. I was thinking what a lonely picture that conjures up—a little girl, all on her own, riding all day up there.' He gestured to the gently rolling hills, but then, sensing his glance rest on her, she shrugged slightly.

'Well, I was an only child. They're always lonely, aren't they? Oh, good,' as they rounded the path in the shrubbery, she pointed to where a dark blue Daimler stood on the gravel, 'Dad's back. Thank goodness for that. I was afraid——'

She broke off, and Nick, his brows raised, prompted, 'Afraid he wouldn't get back? But surely, on New Year's Eve——'

'Yes, well,' she mumbled, 'he's very busy, you know, so he's away a lot. Come on. I want you to meet him.' And she tugged him across the lawn and in through the side entrance.

She walked in ahead of Nick, then, in the hall, under the shadow of the huge balustraded staircase, came to an abrupt halt, her hand to her mouth. On the landing, directly overhead, she heard her parents' low, angry voices and her stomach clenched against the familiar hurt.

'So you've deigned to come back.' Her mother's voice, quietly venomous. 'We *are* honoured!'

Her father muttered something which Carly did not quite catch, then his wife laughed, an unmusical sound.

'Don't give me that, Richard. Go to London on business, on New Year's Eve? You couldn't keep away from the little tart even for a few days, could you?'

'Shut up, damn you!' Her father's voice was tight with anger. 'Maybe I wouldn't stay away if you weren't quite such a cold-blooded fish.'

Carly, the man behind her quite forgotten, closed her eyes as the old panic, the old pain gripped her. Dimly, she felt Nick's arm go round her, but when she looked up dazedly she saw the compassion in his eyes and shook it off fiercely.

'No, I won't shut up, as you so charmingly put it. If you care nothing for me, what about your only daughter? She's arrived, with some——'

Carly's brain propelled her into action. Banging the door to behind them, she advanced into the well of the hall.

'Come on, Nick.' Her voice was a hollow mockery of itself. 'Time to change for the party.'

At the foot of the stairs she halted and looked up, her face very pale. 'Hello, Daddy. Did you have a good trip?'

'Carly, my pet! Lovely to see you.'

'Hello, Zoë.' Pinning back the smile, which had slipped a little, Carly made room on the brocade sofa for one of her mother's bridge friends.

'What a gorgeous brute,' said Zoë. 'Wherever did you find him?'

'Mr Bradley, you mean?' she said carefully. 'He owns the foundry in Milton where I work two days a week.'

'Oh, of course—Jane mentioned something about it. Lucky you!'

The older woman's small blue eyes gave her a quick, speculative glance, then returned to Nick, who was standing across the other side of the room, glass in hand, talking to a group of men, Carly's father among them.

Carly glanced sideways at the woman beside her, and saw Zoë's face, carefully made up to disguise the ravages of two bitterly fought divorces and a long career in the saddle, watching Nick with the look of a predatory animal. Not knowing whether to be amused or repelled, she switched her gaze back to Nick.

How handsome he was... Whatever he wore—whether it was old faded jeans or, as now, immaculate evening dress, it was with a casual panache. As she watched, he said something to her father, making him roar with laughter. At least they seemed to be hitting it off. Well, that wasn't really surprising, now she thought about it. They had quite a lot in common—both highly successful self-made men, who delighted in their flair for tough wheeler-dealing—and both of them, she realised with a sense of shock, exuded the same kind of almost animal vitality, which seemed to be barely contained within their smooth exteriors.

As if sensing her gaze on him, Nick glanced across at her, flashing her a half-smile that seemed to hold a secret message, just for her, and she felt a little warming glow, then a sudden twist of desire. Conscious of Zoë's eyes, shrewdly assessing, on her, she looked away, only to see that her mother was also watching the two men, her lips pursed.

Had she also caught Nick's look, read the message in his eyes? And had she, like Carly herself, sensed the similarities in the two men? If so, it was another black mark for Nick... Had there ever been any love between her parents, she wondered miserably, any passion such as she and Nick had shared last night? If so, it had soon burnt itself out... But then maybe it always did—and especially within the bounds of marriage. She only had to look around this room to see that.

Zoë was still watching her. Carly stood up abruptly. 'Let me get you another drink, Zoë. Same again?'

As she turned away one of her father's business associates bumped into her, narrowly missing shedding his glass of whisky all over her.

''Lo, Carly, m'dear.'

'Hello, Dan.'

'Wonderful party.' His voice was ever so slightly slurred. 'Still, never known a duff one at the Manor yet, eh?'

Carly smiled politely and slipped past as, with a 'Hi there, Zoë. As gorgeous as ever, I see,' he dropped into her vacated seat.

It was true, of course, what he'd said. Never anything but wonderful parties here. In fact that, looking back, was what her growing up had been; desperately trying to close her ears to her parents tearing one another apart and then, just hours later, watching them put on yet another superb show of togetherness. They really should get an Oscar, she thought, with a savage stab of pain, and went to get Zoë's gin and tonic refilled.

At last it was over. The last balloons had been popped...the last champagne toasts drunk...the last salmon canapés...foie gras...caviare downed.

Carly had ached to retreat into the seclusion of the conservatory with Nick, but he'd seemed intent on playing the Good Guest to the end, only chatting to her in between another round of circulating. Only when they'd all joined hands in a giant circle all around the ground floor, to sing 'Auld Lang Syne' as the church clock faintly struck midnight, had he materialised and held her hand tightly in his, then, in the general mêlée, taken her in his arms and kissed her with an almost angry intensity.

But then, as the last guests filtered away, she found herself alone with him in the porch.

'Nick, please,' she clutched his hand, 'come to my room tonight—or I'll come to yours.'

All at once, she felt a desperate need of the reassurance of his arms, but he shook his head wryly.

'No, my sweet. I have a feeling your mother intends spending what's left of the night on patrol between our rooms. I'd hate to give her any more reason for detesting me—or, much worse, to embarrass you. But tomorrow—or rather,' his voice dropped to an intimate whisper, his eyes dark with promise, 'tonight, once we're safely back in Milton——'

He left the sentence unfinished as they heard her father's voice from the hall. His lips brushed hers, and he was gone.

'You're quite sure you can't stay any longer, darling?'

'I'm sorry, Mummy.' Carly leaned across the breakfast table to give her mother's hand a little squeeze. 'But—well, Nick has to be back tomorrow morning——'

'Ah, yes, the *foundry*.' Mrs Sheppard looked as though she had discovered the word in her mouth and did not quite know what to do with it. 'Roger will be so sorry to have missed you, dear. He couldn't make it to the party last night—although, of course, he wasn't to know that you'd be there.' She turned to Nick. 'Roger and Caroline have been such good friends for years.'

Nick inclined his head politely, but not before Carly had caught the faint gleam of amusement in his eyes.

'Now, if you'll excuse me a moment,' Mrs Sheppard pushed back her chair and stood up, 'I want a word with Ellen.'

As she disappeared in the direction of the kitchen, Nick said drily, 'And who might Roger be, then?'

'Oh,' Carly gave him a rueful smile, 'he's the son of old family friends. Mummy made up her mind when I was four that if I ever were to get married, he'd make ideal husband material. I gave up long ago trying to convince her that I just don't see him that way.'

'But in any case he's a useful "Keep off the Grass" sign to ward off any unwelcome intruders.'

'Something like that, yes. But, Nick,' she went on urgently, 'don't let her rile you, please. We'll be away soon.'

'I'll try—although,' a smile flickered across his face for a moment, 'I'd love to crack that cool exterior, just once.'

'No, Nick, you'd only regret it if you did.'

'I might get the same treatment as your father, you mean?' When she winced involuntarily, he reached across and took her hand in his. 'Sorry. Oh, God, Carly,' he went on softly, 'how long has this been going on?'

She didn't need to ask what he meant. 'Oh, as long as I can remember, I suppose.'

'Well, why the hell haven't they divorced?' Nick's face was flushed and she was surprised by the anger vibrating in his voice.

'I don't know, really. They depend on one another, of course, and maybe, in spite of all appearances, there is something keeping them together. I don't know—how can anyone know,' she gave him a small, bitter smile, 'least of all their daughter?'

Carly was just going downstairs with her overnight bag when her father, pale and rather drawn-looking, emerged from his dressing-room.

She hugged him. 'We're just off. Bye, Daddy. Don't bother to come down.'

He kissed her on the cheek. 'Take care of yourself, my pet. That young man—what's his name? Nick.'

'Y-yes?' she asked fearfully.

'Seems a good lad. I like him.'

'Oh, Daddy!' She smiled at him, then, as Nick appeared at the far end of the corridor, went on down, leaving him to make his farewells.

On the drive, Nick handed her into the car, then, as she watched, she saw her mother extend her fingertips to shake hands. He swung himself in beside her, switched on the ignition, then, as if on an afterthought, wound down his window.

'Oh, by the way, Mrs Sheppard——'

'Yes?' Politely enquiring.

'Have you got your social diary handy?'

'My——? Well, yes, it's in the hall.'

'Good. Would you make a note to keep free—let me see—when do you think, Carly?' As he turned to her, she could only look back at him in blank incomprehension. 'Well, let's say the last weekend in January. I'll be marrying your daughter then.'

And, as he put his foot down on the accelerator, the car roared off across the gravel, with Carly's last view of her mother, transfixed, horror and disbelief struggling in equal measure on her face.

She realised that, beside her, Nick was laughing out loud. 'Well, I think I succeeded, don't you?'

'You idiot!' Half vexed, half laughing, Carly swung round on him. 'You realise Mummy thought you were serious, don't you? Whatever am I going to tell her?'

'You can tell her I was serious.'

Her stomach lurched violently. 'B-but you can't have been!'

'Why not?' Nick had turned out into the narrow lane and was giving all his attention to overtaking a bakery van. 'It was, I grant you, a fairly original way of proposing.'

'P-proposing? You mean you really didn't say it just to annoy her? But you must have done.' Carly felt as if she was going to burst into tears.

'I was never more serious in my life, Carly. Of course, if you prefer a more conventional approach, I can always pull into this farm gateway and go down on one knee.'

'You mean——' her mind was struggling ineffectually to assimilate this devastating turn of events '—you want——'

'To marry you? Yes, I do.'

Carly's hands clutched together in her lap. 'Marry?' she repeated stupidly, and saw Nick's mouth twist.

'You make it sound like a dirty word!'

'But I shall never marry.'

He took one look at her face, then pulled on to the grass verge and cut the engine with a vicious click.

'All right, I apologise. Maybe I shouldn't have done it that way, but I just couldn't resist it. But, Carly——' he tried to take her hand, but she jerked it away '—I'd already made up my mind I was going to propose to you today.'

Blind, unreasoning panic was taking her over, so that she had to resist the impulse to jump out of the car and run away. 'You—you're treating me just like one of your business clients,' she burst out. 'Trying to drive me into a corner, so that I can't say no.'

'And is that what you want to say?'

'Yes, of course it is.'

'Any particular reason?'

'I've told you,' she said stubbornly. 'I don't want to get married.'

'So you're happy to settle for an affair, are you?' Nick said harshly. 'Or maybe I'm flattering myself—was that night at the cottage just a one-night stand?'

'No—no, of course not, but——'

Her voice trailed away, as she realised with a sense of shock that she had not given any really serious thought to how their relationship was going to develop. Perhaps it was that, so cynical as she was about all relationships between men and women, she had deliberately closed her mind to the future and had merely snatched with unthinking gratitude at the magic of the moment.

Nick's voice broke brutally into her silence. 'Well, I'm not willing to settle for anything less. For me, it's marriage or nothing.'

'But—why?'

'Because I love you.'

'What?' The quiet words stunned her, so that at first she could only stare at him, her eyes enormous with shock. 'Oh, no, Nick—please!' She ground her nails into her palms. 'I'm—I'm very fond of you. There's no one I'd rather be with——'

'Many thanks for the unsolicited testimonial!'

'But you must see, I—I—— You can't love me,' she said desperately.

He smiled faintly. 'My darling girl, I've loved you since the first time I saw you. Oh, I know I told you I'd wanted you from the day you first walked into my office, but that was only a part of it. As you drove away from the car park that night, I swore that, come what may, I'd get you for my own.'

'Yes.' She clung on despairingly to the straw he had unwisely held out to her. 'You wanted me—so you took me. But you don't love me—not at all.' Relief was surging through her.

'I love you.' He turned her face to his so that she had to look into his eyes, and what she saw there made her throat contract with fear.

'What's the matter, Carly?' His lips thinned into a bitter smile. 'Is such an idea too much for you to cope with? Maybe you're only capable of accepting love from a bunch of kids, after all. Is the love of a grown man so terrifying?'

Yes—yes, it is, she wanted to scream, but instead managed somehow to meet his eyes unwaveringly, although she could not speak.

'Of course, I understand now what's made you the way you are. But, my darling,' she flinched away from the endearment, 'not all marriages are like your parents'.'

'Aren't they?' It was no more than a whisper. 'Zoë—Dan—half the people in that room last night—Rex Sandford, after anything in a skirt.'

'Have you forgotten my parents?' Nick's face was strained. 'They were blissfully happy for nearly forty years.'

'Yes, and look at your father now.' Her voice shook. 'You told me yourself he'll never get over losing her, that he's aged ten years since she died.'

'But I think if you asked him he'd say that he would accept that gladly in return for what he'd gained.' There was a long silence, but when at last she looked up at his set face he went on sombrely, 'Without pain, Carly, there is no joy. Until you accept that, accept the risks of opening yourself up to possible pain, there can be no real lasting joy, either.'

The dead hand of despair was clutching at her. 'Well, in that case, I think I'd rather do without the joy,' she said slowly. 'So—so this is the end for us, Nick?' Her ashen lips could barely frame the words.

He caught her hand between his own, crushing it so tightly that she almost cried out, then set it down again.

'I've told you, I love you. The only thing I want is to have you with me all the time, for the rest of my life. But you can't take that, can you, Carly?'

His words flayed her. She wanted to slide to the floor, dissolving into helpless tears of misery. Instead, she set her chin proudly.

'I don't choose to tie myself to a man, no.'

Nick, his face as pale as marble, restarted the car and without even glancing in his mirror, jabbed his foot hard down on the accelerator and swung back out into the lane.

CHAPTER TWELVE

THE man finished driving in the post. He peered through the sheeting rain, saw Carly at the kitchen window and gave her a quick thumbs-up, then sprinted across to his van and disappeared in a cloud of spray.

Still, though, she did not move, but stood gazing listlessly out, past the clumps of gold and blue crocuses which were grimly defying the March weather, to the board. And even when she finally roused herself to turn back to the sink, the red 'FOR SALE' letters seemed to burn in her brain.

The dishes did not take long. This morning, as so often, she hadn't really been hungry and had settled for coffee and a slice of toast. Perhaps that was what was wrong with her—she simply wasn't eating enough. Or maybe—she looked out of the window again—it was the prospect of a wet Saturday, to be followed by an equally wet Sunday...

All at once, as though unable to bear the silence a moment longer, she turned on her heel, snatched up her mac and bag, and drove off into town.

She returned two hours later. Putting all the groceries she had bought—and would almost certainly never eat—into the larder or the fridge, she went upstairs, took the new skirt and sweater from their bags and put them away in the wardrobe, without even holding them up to herself.

But at least she'd got out of this silent house for a while, and now she felt able to fetch her pile of college exercise books and sit down at the kitchen table. The work, though, which once upon a time would have engrossed her for hours, now seemed tedious, measured by the tick of the clock on the wall behind her, and once again, as so often these last few weeks, she caught herself thinking, Thank goodness this term is nearly over!

What a term it had been... That first morning, back in January, she'd gone to see Dr Jutson and asked to be released from her shadowing at Bradley's. Oh, she'd had her story nicely worked out. She'd learned all she could about foundry work... any more sessions there would just be a waste of time... It would make much more sense for her to complete her stint in another type of firm altogether... The rimless glasses had given her a long, cold look, then agreed, and, in a kind of numbed stupor she had found herself spending her Mondays and Tuesdays since then in a cotton mill in the next valley.

Somehow, she'd gone on living. And not just living, but teaching, walking, talking, smiling—while all the time she knew that behind the mask, which she never allowed to slip even a fraction, she was withering away.

Just once, in all this bleak term, had she been jolted into reality. Hurrying through town late one snowy afternoon, she had suddenly come face to face with Nick. As though turned to stone, she'd stopped dead, her hand flying instinctively to her throat.

He seemed to hesitate momentarily, then said, his voice clipped, 'Are you all right?'

'Oh, yes—yes, I'm fine.' She'd even managed the facsimile of a confident smile.

'You're not—you don't need any help from me?'

Colour washed through her face as realisation hit her. 'Oh, there's no need for you to worry,' she said proudly. 'No, I'm not pregnant.'

'Ah.' Nick had seemed about to speak again, but then, with the merest of nods, had walked on.

Carly had stood for a moment, her shoulders bowed as though from some terrible grief, then straightened herself and continued along the pavement.

Back at the cottage at last, she'd stared, heavy-eyed, at herself in the mirror. That split-second meeting had forced her to face herself, and what she had done—what she had promised herself she would never, ever do. She had allowed a man to breach those painfully constructed fortifications around herself.

But somehow she had to rebuild that wall—and even higher this time. After all, it was possible to get over any man, wasn't it? It was just a matter of time. And the summer was coming. Maybe she'd go abroad for a couple of weeks, and then in September she'd be picking up her new 3S class. A new class, a new start.

It had been just over a week ago when Dr Jutson had sent for her and announced that, as from September, he was disbanding the remedial department and dispersing its students through the rest of the forms. So there would be no 3S.

Carly had gone home that evening and considered her future in the curiously detached way she'd developed lately, as though she were planning someone else's life. Next morning, she'd handed in her notice to take effect from July, put her cottage in the hands of a local estate agent, and began job-hunting by ordering *The Times Educational Supplement*, the latest copy of which lay still unopened in the next room.

She continued marking through to the afternoon, then finally pushed away the last set of books, pressing her fingers to her aching eyes. It was too late for lunch, but she made a pot of tea, nibbling some biscuits as she waited for the kettle, then took the tray into the sitting-room.

Here at the back of the house the wind was whistling around the eaves. To drown it, she switched on the radio, tuning to the local station. Only half listening, she finished her biscuits, then, as she brushed the crumbs from her lap, she froze, her hand suspended.

'...Still no news of the four potholers missing since early this morning in the White Scar cave system at Ingleborough.'

Carly heard someone give a choked moan, then felt the spasm of sick terror that physically racked her body.

'...We are now going over to our reporter at the scene, Pam Cook.'

Every fibre of her strung to instant breaking point, Carly stared blank-eyed at the radio.

'Up here the rain is still torrential and the Met. Office forecasts that it will continue at least until this evening. The potholers, who became trapped when the levels of water rose because of the heavy rain overnight, are believed to have been attempting to break through to an until now unexplored system——'

Oh, God—Nick. Please, don't let it be Nick!

'...The group, which includes one woman, are all students at Leeds University.'

'Oh, thank heavens!' It was torn from her lips before, next moment, the searing guilt took over as she thought of the four young people, trapped in the cold darkness.

'...Police, ambulances and rescue services are here and everyone is doing all they can. The rescue operation is well under way, but with more rain——'

Jerkily, Carly switched off the radio and got to her feet. Then as she picked up the tray, she noticed a film of dust on the coffee table. And the yellow bobbles of mimosa which she'd bought a couple of days earlier, in a futile attempt to cheer herself up, were looking grey and dusty. Suppose, in spite of the weather, some prospective purchasers should arrive? Maybe she ought to flick a duster around in here.

Half an hour later she switched off the vacuum cleaner and looked around her critically. The room was back to its usual neat self, and the physical exercise seemed to have done her good. Was there anything else she could do, now she was in the mood? Her eyes strayed to the glass cabinet...Yes, her beloved paperweights—she had neglected them for weeks.

Setting them carefully on the tray, she took them all out to the kitchen and, filling the bowl with warm suds, gently washed each small globe. She'd been right—this familiar action really was very soothing. She had almost finished, when a gust of wind blew a branch of the pear tree against the window, its dry scratching like fingers. 'Let me in...Let me in. I'd lost my way.' The ghostly voice of Heathcliff's dead love——

The paperweight she was holding slid through her wet fingers, to crash on to the quarry-tiled floor. It split, and the two halves lay at her feet.

'No! Oh, no!'

Carly pulled off her rubber gloves and went down on her knees, cradling the pieces in her hands. The girl's face was no longer alight, her fair hair no longer streamed in the wind, and the feather she was reaching for had disappeared in a mesh of crazed glass.

A slow tear rolled down her cheek, then dropped on to the wreckage, followed by another.

What shall I do? What shall I do? Over and over, the words pounded in her mind. Then, as though her senses were bypassing her reason, she sprang to her feet and, snatching down her car keys, ran headlong out of the cottage.

At Nick's house, she flung herself up the steps to the front door, banging on the knocker. Even as she heard footsteps, she thought with a flicker of fear, How will he greet me? Will he rebuff me, with those ice-cold stranger's eyes? But she had to tell him.

The door opened.

'Nick, I——' It was not Nick. It was a grey-haired woman. 'C-can I speak to Mr Bradley?'

'I'm sorry, miss, he isn't here.'

But he had to be—she must tell him!

'Oh, miss!' For the first time, Carly registered the strain on the other woman's face. 'I'm that worried about him!'

'About Nick?' And the sense of chill unease clutched at her.

'There's been no more news for hours. The cave——'

'The cave?' Carly, normally so quick-witted, stared at her blankly, then with dawning horror. 'You mean, those potholers?'

'Yes.'

'But he can't be! It said they're students.'

'He's leading the rescue team. I begged him not to—he hasn't been at all well—but of course I couldn't stop him.'

But you should have done! Carly had to clench her fists in her tracksuit pockets to stop herself beating them against the wall. You should have done—because I love him, and I can't live without him, and if anything's happened to him, how shall I go on living?

'Are you all right, miss? Out without a coat in this weather—you're soaked! Come in and get dry.'

But Carly brushed off her hand as though it were an insect. 'What? Oh, no, thank you. I must go.'

She gave her a caricature of a smile, then ran back through the rain to her car.

Right out here on the moors, she had been afraid she would get lost, but for quite a distance, even in the settling dusk, she had seen the gaggle of vehicles parked off the road along a track.

As she pulled up, a policeman came splashing through the mud. She wound her window down and he leaned in a little, the spears of rain lancing against his cap.

'Press, miss? Your lot are over there.' He jerked his thumb in the direction of a miserable-looking huddle of mackintoshed figures.

'N-no, I'm a friend of Nick—Mr Bradley,' she said quickly, terrified that he would send her away.

'Oh, I see.' Was it her overstretched imagination, or did his expression almost imperceptibly change?

'Is there any news?' She tried to sound matter-of-fact, but her voice cracked.

'Afraid not. We're still trying to re-establish radio contact.' He regarded her kindly. 'Why don't you go and get yourself a nice hot cup of tea? There's a mobile canteen over there, behind that—er—ambulance.' Their eyes met and flickered apart.

'No—no, thank you.' Anything would choke her, or, far worse, loosen up that tight knot in her chest sufficiently to let all the months of waiting tears past. She forced a smile. 'I'll be all right.'

Carly came to with a jerk. For a moment she gazed around her blankly, then her elbow banged against the side of the car. As she rubbed it mechanically, she peered at the car clock. Almost one a.m. On the radio the music which had lulled her to sleep was still playing; she switched it off, then wound down her window, her tired eyes trying to assimilate what was going on.

Floodlights had been fixed up, so that vehicles and faces alike were bathed in an eerie yellow light, but apart from that there was no movement, no sound. The rescue team had been below ground for about eighteen hours. Surely by now—— But her mind shrank away from the direction her thoughts were taking.

All at once, unable to sit hunched in the car a moment longer, she got out, stretching herself, easing stiff muscles. The keen wind cut like a knife through her damp tracksuit, but it freshened her brain after the long hours of stupor.

Hugging her arms to herself, she walked down the path, then halted as she reached the road. When she turned, she could see, against the black sky, the blacker menace of the mountain rearing itself up. Somewhere under there was everything she cared for...

Hardly aware of her surroundings, she tripped against a boulder, almost falling headlong into a tiny, swollen stream, but then she swung round as, behind her, she heard a faint shout.

Next moment people were beginning to move, jumping out from cars and vans, and she was stumbling back down the track. The first black-suited figure was already being supported towards an ambulance when she pulled up, just on the periphery. Her heart leapt, then fell again when the helmet was gently pulled off to reveal fair hair.

A second figure emerged, blinking into the light, then behind him a third man was helped out by two others. Was *he* one of them? No. Desperately Carly tried to read their faces, but nothing, not even relief, showed behind the grime and exhaustion.

The doors of the first ambulance were banged to. It reversed and roared away, its blue light flashing, casting a sickly glow over the men's faces, and the other one pulled into its place, its doors already open.

Drawn by something outside of herself, Carly found herself edging forward, but at a curt, 'Now then, miss, out of the way *please*,' she retreated to the shadows again, her eyes strained on the cave entrance, willing more figures to emerge. The tension around her was becoming almost unbearable; even the radio reporter, who had been chattering excitedly into her tape recorder, fell silent. But at last a ragged cheer broke out and the newspapermen's flashlights flared, as two more figures dragged themselves out—neither one of them, though, the one her eyes were seeking.

And then, quite suddenly, Nick was there. He and another man were easing a narrow stretcher out between them, and strapped tightly to it—Carly could see quite clearly—was a girl, very white, very frightened, very young.

All this she took in in a moment, the rest of her attention fixed hungrily on him. The stretcher was taken from them, and he and the other man straightened up, flexing their backs. As he turned, he lurched against one of the police vans, but when an ambulanceman went to help him he shook off his hand.

Carly was walking towards him. Nick, his face grey, was just taking off his helmet. A white pressure line ran across his brow and there was a graze along one cheekbone, from which blood was oozing.

When he saw her, he went very still. They stood regarding one another for a moment, then Carly, every nerve-ending in her body raw with the tension, and all the things which she had spent the dark hours carefully rehearsing forgotten, laid her head against his mud-caked chest.

'You—you fool!' Suddenly she threw a punch at his stomach. 'Why didn't you tell me?'

'Tell you what?' His voice was hoarse and he made no effort to put his arms round her.

'That you weren't any old p-potholer—that you were in the rescue team.'

He slightly lifted one shoulder. 'Well, I wasn't then. I rejoined in January.'

'Oh.' She lifted her head and looked at him, but his face told her nothing.

'Sorry, Mr Bradley——' a policeman—*her* police-man—put his hand under Nick's elbow '—but we've got to get you to hospital for a check-up.'

But he couldn't be taken away from her, not when she'd just found him again. She clutched at his other arm and Nick, after a quick glance at her face, said, 'I'll be fine—really.' But his eyes were still on Carly. 'I just need a bath and to sleep for a week.'

'Well——' the officer looked from one to the other '—we've got a doctor here. At least let him give you a once-over.' And Nick allowed himself to be led away.

He turned back to her once. 'Wait for me, Carly.' It was a question, and in reply she nodded dumbly. All my life, my darling.

She watched as the two men walked across to one of the police vans and climbed in, then she went back to her own car. Gradually the operation was running down. The second ambulance jolted off down the track, followed by the police cars, and one by one the arc lights were switched off.

But still she saw Nick, changed into his jeans and sweater, coming towards her. She got out, shivering, and waited for him. He came up to her and stood looking down at her.

'You're still here, then?'

'Of course. Didn't you expect me to be?' Her voice trembled.

In the dim light she felt rather than saw a faint smile. 'I don't know. I wondered back there whether, after nearly eighteen hours underground, I was hallucinating.'

She put both hands against his chest. 'I'm here, Nick. Alive—and warm. At least,' as her teeth chattered uncontrollably, 'not very warm, but——'

'Get in.' He seized her roughly by the arms and bundled her back into the Mini, then squeezed his large frame in beside her.

In the dim glow from the interior light they regarded one another unsmilingly.

'Oh, Nick.' Her lip quivered and she bit on it hard. 'I thought you were——' Unable to go on, she could only shake her head.

'Carly,' his voice was strained, 'this isn't just some emotional overreaction, something you'll bitterly regret in daylight?'

'No, Nick, it isn't,' she said urgently. He must believe her! 'Before your housekeeper told me that you were— down there, I knew.'

'Knew what?'

She wanted him to reach out and take her in his arms, but he only watched her, his face expressionless.

'What an utter fool I've been.' She picked at a snag in her tracksuit. 'You were right—what you said. I see it now. About the joy and the pain—when you love someone, I mean. Although,' she managed a pallid smile, 'you've given me enough pain these last few hours to do me quite a while!'

'Oh, my poor love!' At last Nick reached for her, but she held him off for a moment.

'And I must tell you—that beautiful paperweight you bought me, and you said the girl looked like me—well, I broke it!' Her face crumpled and putting her head in her hands she burst into sobs.

'Oh, my darling, don't!' He gathered her to him. 'Never mind the wretched paperweight. I'll buy you fifty more.'

He hushed her, stroking her hair, until at last the sobs subsided, then he held her away from him, wiping away the last tears. 'Sure?' There was still a faint shadow in his eyes.

She gave him a blurred smile. 'Perfectly, perfectly sure. I love you. I've loved you—oh, since the very first day I flounced into your office.'

Then, at last, he laughed and held her to him again.

'Promise me one thing,' she murmured into the folds of wool.

'Anything.'

'That you'll teach me to pothole.'

'Oh, no!' He sounded aghast. 'You'd hate it.'

'But I'll hate far more waiting for you to come back,' Carly said simply.

'Well, I'll have to give that some thought. It may be simpler all round for me to give up. But don't let's talk about that tonight,' he said as she tried to argue. 'I had to promise the doctor back there that you'd take me home and fuss over me like a mother hen with one chick.'

'Oh, I'll do that.' The love and happiness shimmered on her face, and putting up her hand, she gently stroked the graze on his cheek. 'A hot bath, a long sleep, and then what do you say to roast beef and Yorkshire pudding?'

'Perfect.' Their eyes met in a shared smile. 'You know, it's a pity we missed that date in January. Think of all those wonderful Sunday lunches I could have been having since then.'

'So you only want me for my cordon bleu cooking,' she pouted. 'Well, that's very nice to know!'

'No, Carly.' Nick smiled again, but his dark eyes were serious. 'I'm marrying you because you're the most fascinating——' he leaned forward and kissed the tip of her nose '—gorgeous——' he kissed one eyebrow '—desirable——' and the other '—thoroughly infuriating young woman I'm ever likely to meet.' And finally his lips came down on hers.

'Oh, Nick,' she said dreamily, several minutes later, 'let's get married tomorrow.'

'No.' He shook his head determinedly. 'It's Easter in three weeks, and I think that would be a very nice time of year for you to marry me.'

'Oh, yes, Nick.' She was so full of happiness that she could barely speak. 'An Easter wedding would be perfect, my darling.'

Hi,
Italy, as always, is
a model's paradise.
But I'm tired of the
obligatory parties,
the devouring eyes.
Particularly those
of Nicolo Sabatini,
who seems to think
I should be for his
eyes only.
            Love, Caroline

Take 4 bestselling love stories FREE

Plus get a FREE surprise gift!

HARLEQUIN®
PRESENTS Plus

Meet Matt Hunter. He doesn't recognize that Nicola, his new assistant, is the woman who shared his bed one night, eight long years ago. Hardly flattering, but then Nicola has no intention of reminding him of the occasion!

And then there's Grant Goodman. He *must* know about Briony's past, but it hasn't stopped him from hiring her to manage his newest resort in Tasmania. And it may explain his sordid propositions—which Briony could easily ignore if she didn't find Grant so attractive!

Matt and Grant are just two of the sexy men you'll fall in love with each month in Harlequin Presents Plus.

Don't miss

Past Passion by Penny Jordan
Harlequin Presents Plus #1655

and

Unwilling Mistress by Lindsay Armstrong
Harlequin Presents Plus #1656

Harlequin Presents Plus
The best has just gotten better!

Available in June wherever Harlequin books are sold.

PPLUS13

**This June, Harlequin invites
you to a wedding of**

Promised Brides

Celebrate the joy and romance of weddings past with
PROMISED BRIDES—a collection of original historical short
stories, written by three best-selling historical authors:

> *The Wedding of the Century*—MARY JO PUTNEY
> *Jesse's Wife*—KRISTIN JAMES
> *The Handfast*—JULIE TETEL

Three unforgettable heroines, three award-winning authors!
PROMISED BRIDES is available in June wherever Harlequin
Books are sold.

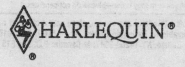

HARLEQUIN®

HARLEQUIN®

Don't miss these Harlequin favorites by some of our most
distinguished authors!
And now, you can receive a discount by ordering two or more titles!

HT #25551	THE OTHER WOMAN by Candace Schuler	$2.99	☐
HT #25539	FOOLS RUSH IN by Vicki Lewis Thompson	$2.99	☐
HP #11550	THE GOLDEN GREEK by Sally Wentworth	$2.89	☐
HP #11603	PAST ALL REASON by Kay Thorpe	$2.99	☐
HR #03228	MEANT FOR EACH OTHER by Rebecca Winters	$2.89	☐
HR #03268	THE BAD PENNY by Susan Fox	$2.99	☐
HS #70532	TOUCH THE DAWN by Karen Young	$3.39	☐
HS #70540	FOR THE LOVE OF IVY by Barbara Kaye	$3.39	☐
HI #22177	MINDGAME by Laura Pender	$2.79	☐
HI #22214	TO DIE FOR by M.J. Rodgers	$2.89	☐
HAR #16421	HAPPY NEW YEAR, DARLING		
	by Margaret St. George	$3.29	☐
HAR #16507	THE UNEXPECTED GROOM by Muriel Jensen	$3.50	☐
HH #28774	SPINDRIFT by Miranda Jarrett	$3.99	☐
HH #28782	SWEET SENSATIONS by Julie Tetel	$3.99	☐

Harlequin Promotional Titles

#83259	UNTAMED MAVERICK HEARTS	$4.99	☐
	(Short-story collection featuring Heather Graham Pozzessere, Patricia Potter, Joan Johnston)		

(limited quantities available on certain titles)

	AMOUNT	$
DEDUCT:	10% DISCOUNT FOR 2+ BOOKS	$
	POSTAGE & HANDLING	$
	($1.00 for one book, 50¢ for each additional)	
	APPLICABLE TAXES*	$ _____
	TOTAL PAYABLE	$ _____
	(check or money order—please do not send cash)	

To order, complete this form and send it, along with a check or money order for the
total above, payable to Harlequin Books, to: **In the U.S.:** 3010 Walden Avenue,
P.O. Box 9047, Buffalo, NY 14269-9047; **In Canada:** P.O. Box 613, Fort Erie, Ontario,
L2A 5X3.

Name: _____

Address: _____ City: _____

State/Prov.: _____ Zip/Postal Code: _____

*New York residents remit applicable sales taxes.
Canadian residents remit applicable GST and provincial taxes.

HBACK-AJ